About the author

Mo Tritton lived in East London with her Staffie dog, some rabbits and a couple of budgies. She is fascinated by and loves bees, especially the many varieties of solitary bees.

She always had a vivid imagination and scribbled ideas on bits of paper but did not start writing seriously till in her sixties as she did not believe in herself.

She loves motorcycles, especially British ones, for the unique feeling of freedom they give.

Her bucket list includes watching starlings murmuring, getting a few bee hives, having a book serialised on television et al. The list keeps growing.

Also by the Author

A Slice of Life
Blaze of Glory

SHADOWZZZZZ

Mo Tritton

SHADOWZZZZZ
Part 1 of a Trilogy

Vanguard Press

VANGUARD PAPERBACK

© Copyright 2024
Mo Tritton

A CIP catalogue record for this title is
available from the British Library.

ISBN 978-1-80016-483-3

*Vanguard Press is an imprint of
Pegasus Elliot Mackenzie Publishers Ltd.*
www.pegasuspublishers.com

First Published in 2024

**Vanguard Press
Sheraton House Castle Park
Cambridge England**

Printed & Bound in Great Britain

Dedication

I love wolves with a passion and believe they should not need human approval to live their lives in a natural way.

List of Characters

B4U—Shadow to Bear's mother.

B212—Shadow who tried to exchange places with 4Z9.

DRT4—Shadow to Mosaic.

FLR2/A1—Shadow to young girl in the squat.

K04—Shadow to the Prime Minister.

R1—Shadow to Apache the rabbit.

R45N—Maisie, Bear's wife's shadow.

R4T+—Sparkle's shadow.

RS2—Shadow to salesperson.

RZ2R—Roy, Maisie's son's shadow.

X81—Shadow who replaced ZUP2.

Z8—Shadow at seance.

ZUP2—Shadow to Daisy (wants to join the S.A.S.)

37—Shadow to Bear's father then an albatross.

88T—Shadow to Maisie's mum.

4Z9—Shadow without a human who was a gang leader.

Charlie—Shadow to Bear.

YEW2 - Tree near statue in London

PC1 - former Prime Minister shadow

Chief - Commander of all shadows

MST3 - shadow to Shimmer

S.A.S. - Shadow Authenticity Squad

P.A.T.H. - Progress attained through Humility

R7 - shadow to Legolas the rabbit

Foreword

Charlie is a shadow, who up until now dislikes the human he is a shadow to and spends as little time as possible attached to him. Whilst talking to a tutor, Charlie is told that if he doesn't start looking after his human, he could be sentenced to spending a long time as a shadow to a still life object.

Jolted into reality, Charlie tried to make amends and help his human become enlightened though he has to find out what being enlightened means. He meets shadows who have become animal shadows and decides that that is what he wants more than anything.

Along the way, he comes into contact with the S.A.S. (shadow authenticity squad) as they battle against a shadow who wants to make an impact in both the shadow and human worlds.

Chapter 1 — Inanimate object

Charlie was bored with sitting in class hearing the same old thing (or so it seemed) over and over again. He looked around at his classmates astounded that they seemed to be paying attention. He tried to distract a shadow sitting next to him but didn't succeed so tuned in again to the teacher just in case she was saying anything important.

"—and if you get it right this time, if you show that you have really learned from mistakes made in previous lives you will—"

Charlie tuned out again and sighed, why on earth did they keep repeating the stuff he'd heard before, why didn't they tell them something they didn't know.

He decided to ask a question and put his hand up to get attention, then, when signalled to do so he asked his question, "Miss, why do some people die before they are born, it's not fair that the shadows assigned to them don't have to do anything, is it?"

Although Charlie was bored with hearing the same old things from the teacher time and time again, he repeated the same old question to them time and time again as it was never answered to his satisfaction.

The teacher responded by saying, "Those students who were assigned did not know at the time that their chosen human was never going to be born, was never going to live on the earth. They were exemplary in carrying out their preparations and that is the reason that they are in line to be in human form for this incarnation if they wish to be."

"So why haven't I been assigned to one of them then?"

"To answer your question, Charlie, you haven't been assigned a miscarried or stillborn human because you are not good enough to do so. You are still looking for the easy way out with as little involvement as possible."

"If I was told that they were going to die before they were born, I would be," Charlie blurted out thoroughly believing what he was saying.

The teacher sighed deeply. "You are missing the point, Charlie, no shadow knows when their human is going to die. They have to be seen to be doing the best they can from the moment they are assigned a human who is developing in the womb. If they are just hanging around waiting for their human to die that is not doing the best they can, is it?"

Some of the students from class were leaving as their humans were beginning to waken. Charlie watched them disappear and knew that he should be going also as he felt his human beginning to stir but he resisted the urge to leave, after all, as he had told the teacher many times before, shadows weren't needed indoors, who noticed that they didn't have a shadow when they went indoors, in fact who noticed they had shadows anyway! Shadows had for far too long been taken for granted and it wasn't fair!

Charlie felt that it was usually only when humans went outdoors into the light that their shadow had to be with them, though not if it was a cloudy, overcast day, and it very much looked as if today was going to be overcast.

The class teacher collected her stuff and made way for the next teacher who was teaching shadows whose humans had worked on a night shift, giving him a tight smile as he passed her.

She turned to Charlie and said, "We need to talk," and headed off without checking that Charlie was following her. He was, as he dared not upset her or any of the teachers if it comes to that.

"What's the problem, Charlie?"

Charlie shrugged his shoulders and looked down at the floor but said nothing.

"Why aren't you looking after your human is the question I should be asking and you should be responding to," she said in a much firmer tone to let him know that silence wasn't an option.

"He's so boring, he's a slob. All he does is drink, eat and sleep."

"So whose fault is that then?" the teacher asked pointedly.

"I know, you're going to say it's mine, my fault, but I have tried, really I have," Charlie lied, unable to look in her face as he was doing so.

His teacher looked at him but said nothing and eventually Charlie wilted under her constant stare and looked up at her. "I'm just fed up with being a shadow to a useless human, that's all."

"Charlie, when you were human, you were cruel and heartless towards other humans—"

Charlie interrupted her. "That's not fair, just because my shadow wasn't doing their job properly, I get the blame."

His teacher looked directly at him pinning his gaze to hers. "Your shadow was doing their job properly but you refused to follow their lead. You refused to admit that you were ever in the wrong and now you think you can get justice by blaming your failure on your shadow! You need to accept that it was you who was to blame. You dealt out rough justice to your fellow humans and totally ignored the gut feelings instigated by your shadow."

Charlie didn't have an answer, after all he knew she was right, he had been a right bastard when he was a human and had ended his days loudly going insane in a prison cell. For a brief moment he thought of his shadow at the time and felt sad for him because he too was a prisoner, it couldn't have been easy for him. He shook off the thought, his teacher was getting to him in more ways than one. His shadow when he had been human was to blame and that was that!

The teacher watched his face and read his thoughts and sighed deeply. In a much softer tone asked him what the responsibilities of a shadow were.

"A shadow has to be responsible for their human twenty-four-seven all their human's life. A human without a shadow lives on the very edge of life, unable to commit to anything, unable to mix with fellow humans but frightened of being on their own. A shadow's purpose is to ensure the health and safety of their human and to make sure that they provide opportunities for the human to learn so that they eventually earn the right to go to a higher place," Charlie finished, breathless as he recited from rote all in one breath.

"What do you mean by saying 'earn the right' to go to a higher place?"

"The human has to show, sometimes through many lifetimes that he has overcome his ego and pride, that he loves his fellow humans and has a genuine heart." Charlie couldn't quite remember the lessons he had learnt by rote so long ago but he thought that he had the gist of them.

"It is the responsibility of the shadow to serve. A shadow must attend classes regularly for study and assessment purposes whilst their human is resting but must always be on the alert for when their human wakes up. Until a shadow learns to truly fulfil his role and becomes selfless, he will always remain a shadow."

Charlie shuffled his feet uncomfortably and sighed hoping to get the teacher on side by his dejected look but he was unlucky, she had seen him try and get around her too many times before.

She waited for him to realise his play acting wasn't getting him anywhere then chilled him by saying, "Buck your ideas up Charlie or you will be downgraded to become the shadow of an inanimate object."

Horrified, Charlie despatched himself back to his human who was wandering about aimlessly trying to find a clean pair of socks to put on. Charlie watched him for a moment or two and felt the same old dissatisfaction creeping back in but shook the feeling from his head. Although the teacher had seemed relatively calm, she had issued a final warning to him and he had better take notice. A few of his friends had been made shadows of inanimate objects and could remain so for hundreds perhaps thousands of years. He went to see them every now and then but found it difficult each time he visited because his friends of old were now different shadows and he wasn't too sure if he even liked them any more, they seemed so repentant.

Charlie attached himself to his human as his human was putting his sock and shoes on then his human ambled out of his house and set off to go to the local pub the same as he had been doing for years, on the way, passing the local park. To his surprise, he found his human turning back and entering the park which he had only been in when his mother took him there as a child. His human had deliberately avoided going into the park since his mother had died suddenly when he was twelve years old because his memories were too painful. She had been a fun person, always laughing and finding good things to say about people, nothing like his dad was now. He thought of his father as a miserable old sod without a good word to say about anybody. Sitting down on a park bench he watched the autumn leaves dress the ground like a blanket, the trees heroically shedding them to face the winter without their protection. He decided that he liked this fact about trees, their selflessness and instead of going to the pub he continued to survey the natural world around him and wonder at it. It was as if his eyes had been opened and he was seeing for the first time what had always been there.

It was getting dark as Charlie's human made his way back from the park and as he passed an even darker alleyway that ran parallel to some shops and served as a delivery lane, Charlie saw a group of shadows laughing and joking and emulating the actions of a local prostitute who was busy servicing a customer. Although Charlie knew his human couldn't see the shadows, he would be able to see the prostitute and her customer if he but glanced that way so Charlie focused all his attention on his human to make sure he kept looking straight ahead.

He recognised some of the shadows as those he usually hung around with and some of them even beckoned him over but he shook his head and walked back home with his human.

"I suppose you've been drinking again," was the greeting his human got from his father who was sitting by the fireplace, a plaid blanket draped around his shoulders and across his knees.

"No, I've been to the park all day actually," his human responded as he took off his coat and scarf and hung them up then. Rubbing his palms briskly together, he moved over to the fireplace and held them out to capture some of the warmth.

His father hadn't been expecting this response and was taken by surprise at his son's sobriety and bit back on the same old cutting remark he usually greeted his son with.

"You eaten?"

"Had a tin of soup, can't chew as having trouble with my teeth," his father volunteered. He didn't like showing any sort of weakness to his son but he'd said it now so that was that.

When the old man fell asleep in his armchair Charlie detached himself from his human and went in search of the old man's shadow and finally found him sitting up in the attic of all places. Usually he totally ignored him, they were responsible for humans living in the same house but that was no reason for them to get on. The shadows had got used to giving each other a wide berth but now Charlie was beginning to see that he should at least try and get on with the other shadow and see if they could make their humans more amenable to each other. He didn't know where to start though so just sat beside the other shadow searching for a conversation opener which, in the end, was obvious.

"Hello, my name is Charlie, what's yours?"

To his surprise the shadow next to him started reciting his identification code number comprised of numbers and letters and anything up to a thousand characters in length. Charlie remembered back to the time when he used to cite his ID number off by heart but very much doubted that he could do it now. He mused over the saying he had heard of that 'if you don't use it, you lose it' and thought that in his case at least it was true.

"What would you like to be called?" he asked when the shadow next to him paused for breath midway through his recital.

"37," said the shadow firmly.

"37 is not a name, it's a number," said Charlie blatantly stating the obvious.

"You asked me what I would like to be called and I would like to be called 37," the shadow responded. "Why are you talking to me now, what are you after?"

Charlie though back over the awkward times in the household and said, "I've realised that it's better for our humans if we at least try to get along."

"What made you realise that?"

Charlie began to concoct a story in his head then surprised himself by telling the truth. "A teacher told me that if I don't pull myself together, I could end up being downgraded and become a shadow to a stationery object!"

37 responded, "I would have thought that that was right up your street after all you don't like doing much."

Charlie smarted as the truth hit home. "I've got to turn things around."

37 thought this over for a moment then said, "How come you are called Charlie, haven't you got an ID number?"

Charlie said, "My ID number is 759 characters in length and starts with an F and finishes with a O so that is why I am called Charlie." They both laughed then stayed quiet for a moment. Charlie said, "Do you remember my human's mother's shadow?"

37 turned and looked at him in surprise before saying, "Yes, of course I do. Why?"

"What was she like?"

"She was kind. I learnt a lot from her."

"Yes, but what was she like, apart from being kind, that is?"

"She was very wise and she loved and respected your human's mother."

"What happened to her, you know, when her human died?"

"Don't you remember anything; don't you remember how she tried to get you to look after her son but you ignored her?"

Charlie felt ashamed as he said, "I wasn't a good shadow back then. I thought I was better than my human."

37 responded with, "You are changing Charlie, I can see it. You are trying at least to be a much better shadow now."

"Do you really think so?"

"Yes, I do. The only thing I wish is that we had got to know each other much sooner."

"So do I. Still, we're friends now, aren't we?"

"Yes, of course we are. Your human's mother's shadow was called B4U."

"B4U?"

"Yes. B4U chose to shadow an oak tree instead of becoming human. I'll show you if—wait, I've got to go now, my human needs me." He then vanished downstairs to the front room.

Charlie sat thinking about the approach he had just made and wondered why he hadn't done it before, life in the house would have been so much easier if he had done so, why on earth had he been making life for himself and his human so difficult!

Charlie followed 37 downstairs and saw that he had attached himself to the old man who had woken up and was now busily reading through racing results. Charlie found that his human had become very agitated during the time he had left him and was pacing about picking things up then putting them down again as if he didn't know what to do with himself. Once Charlie had reattached himself his human became calmer and settled down on the sofa and turned on the television with the remote so that he could watch the rugby highlights. Charlie wasn't particularly keen on rugby, he much preferred football but try as he might his human overrode him and didn't change channels.

Whist his human was occupied watching the television, Charlie monitored his vital signs just to check that there was nothing going wrong with him. He hadn't done so for a long time although it was part of his duty as a shadow. He found that his humans blood pressure was high but reasoned that the cause was because the team he supported were losing badly. He was relieved that everything else seemed to be all right so did an internal body scan and was alarmed to find that his human's kidneys were functioning below par. It was his fault; he knew it was. Rather than stay with his human he had left him to get on with his own life and had gone to meet other 'rogue' shadows for a bit of fun although he knew that his human couldn't function properly without him. At the time he couldn't have cared less what his human got up to, feeling that he was a millstone around his neck who was stopping him from doing the things he wanted to do. Now he realised what a downward spiral he had been on and thanked his teacher for bringing him to his senses.

The old man finished with the paper and let his head slip forward as he fell asleep in front of the fire. It was just a few moments later when 37 let out a shriek which jolted Charlie from his thoughts. For a brief moment he didn't know where he was then saw 37 had detached himself from his human and was floating just above him. "What's the matter, what's wrong?"

"My human, he's dead, he's died. What can I do, help me, help me!"

Charlie detached himself from his human and checked the old man. 37 was right, he was dead. As his human was still engrossed in the game, he took 37 up to the loft and got him to calm down.

"Look, I'll get my human to ring the police and the doctors to inform them, there is nothing left for you to do. It was his time to die and he died."

37 was distraught. "Are you sure he's dead, couldn't we revive him."

"No we can't, he's dead. You did the best you could for him whilst he was alive so you can't blame yourself."

"I loved him. I've been with him for ninety-two years. What am I supposed to do now?"

"Look, you can't do anything for him now, your time with him has ended. You will be called up for a review to see how you supported him through his life and maybe, just maybe you may come back as a human if you have done enough."

"A human, I may come back as a human. Do you think so, do you really think so?"

"Well, what I think doesn't really matter, it's what the review thinks that counts."

37 looked dejected so Charlie said, "Look, if they ask me for a character reference, I can put in a good word for you."

Charlie didn't think that there was the remotest chance of his being asked for a character reference or a reference of any sort but 37 took heart from what he said.

"Thanks Charlie." His image began to fade until he disappeared altogether leaving Charlie sitting staring at an empty space.

He felt a sudden jolt and quickly took himself downstairs and found that his human was trying to shake his dead father awake whilst shouting at him to wake up. He reattached himself with some difficulty as his human was quite animated and managed to get his human to move away from his father and to phone the police and the doctors surgery.

The surgery was closed so he had to leave a voicemail but he choked on the words. "I think my dad is dead, he won't wake up." And just blubbered into the phone.

Charlie had to work harder than he had ever done in his life to make his human put the phone down and sit on the sofa. His human was crying loudly as tears streamed down his face. Charlie was surprised at the emotion shown as his human had very rarely had a kind word or thought about his father.

A loud knock at the door made Charlie's human start as if in surprise then heave himself up off of the sofa and stumble to the front door.

Ten minutes later he found himself answering a lot of questions to uniformed police officers but he had difficulty in responding to them as the shock of his father's death took hold. He eventually managed to inform the police that he had been watching rugby when his father had died right there beside him in fact.

The police doctor examined the body and pronounced the old man dead then arranged for him to be transported to the mortuary.

The early hours of the morning found Charlie's human sitting staring at the dying fire and feeling sad and lonely. He couldn't understand the feeling as he rarely if ever had spoken to his father and usually avoided being in the same room as he was. He had cried himself dry and now sat on the sofa rocking back and forth and occasionally shouting out to his dad that he loved him.

Charlie had never worked so hard with a human in his life. He had managed to keep his human together when the police where there but now he was struggling. He tried to hypnotize his human, repeating over and over how tired he was feeling and that he should go to bed but it took a long time before he finally managed to activate him.

It was such a release to be able to detach himself and leave for a class even if there was not much time left. It was such a relief to be out of the claustrophobic atmosphere. He had previously seen his human react badly when his mother had died but had not stayed with his human long enough to experience how humans dealt with grief. Instead of staying and supporting him he had gone out galivanting about with his shadow friends for he couldn't deal with the rampant emotions his human expressed.

Humans must know that they didn't really die surely, they must, so what on earth was all the fuss about! On the other hand come to think of it he hadn't realised or even thought about the fact that there was a life after death when he had been a human. He remembered thinking that when you died that was it, caput, so why not live life to the max, do what you want and be done with it.

True, the body humans were in got worn out but it didn't die, it just stopped functioning because the inner light left it, everyone knew that surely!

Charlie realised that being a shadow had opened his mind up to a lot of things that he hadn't known as a human and that it was a major part of his remit to enlighten humans to the true purpose of their lives. He wished that he hadn't wasted his time as a human and inwardly cringed as thoughts of repentance kept flooding his mind. He realised now that his shadow back then had been trying to help him move from the path of destruction to the path of enlightenment but he had crushed such thoughts and wouldn't listen to them. He had wasted a valuable human life and had also been in the process of wasting his present time as a human shadow. Charlie knew that he would have continued to have done so if the old man hadn't died or if he hadn't decided to talk to 37. There was also the warning from the teacher to add to the pot of guilt.

The following night Charlie duly attended a seminar but found it difficult to concentrate as he worried about his human. He suddenly realised that his name was being called and shook himself from his thoughts. The class teacher he had previously spoken to was standing in front of him with a concerned look on her face. When she had Charlie's full attention, she asked him to follow her so that they could talk.

"Is there something I can help you with, Charlie?"

"My human has just lost his father and has become very emotional though I can't understand why as he was not close to his father, I never felt anything in his heart except irritation and frustration. There was never much love for his father in his heart even when he was a child, all the love he had was given to his mother."

The teacher nodded her head and said, "Go on."

"I know that you are going to say that it was my fault that I didn't encourage my human to love his father but I couldn't when I didn't like him either."

The teacher sat silently waiting for Charlie to continue but it took quite a long time for Charlie to continue as he listened to what he was saying and digested the magnitude of it.

With realisation in his voice Charlie said, "It was my fault wasn't it, I allowed my feelings to influence my human. I didn't like his father, so I influenced him not to like him as well."

The teacher said, "Charlie, it is never too late to repent."

"Repent! Is that what I am doing?"

"Yes Charlie, you have opened your heart and have been made aware of your responsibilities."

"Then why do I feel so dreadful?"

"Continue to listen to your heart Charlie. You have a difficult journey ahead of you."

Charlie sat with his head bowed for quite a long time and when he looked up, he found that he was on his own and that there was no sign of his teacher. He contemplated joining in with another lesson but decided against it when he didn't recognise any of the shadows there and made his way back to his human.

Chapter 2 — The cupboard was bare

His human was fast asleep and didn't look like waking although Charlie made a lot of noise, that was one of the abilities that shadows had, they could make themselves heard if they needed. The classes Charlie had attended had given out dire warnings about the misuse of any of their abilities but, of course, some of the shadows took heed and others didn't. There was no point in him attaching himself to his human so he drifted out of the house and into the sunny street thereby becoming a shadow without a human, not that any of the people hurrying by noticed! After a few moments he came across a group of shadows laughing and generally mucking about. He knew most of them but wasn't in the mood to mix with them and would have passed straight by them if he hadn't been seen and approached by some of them.

"Hi Charlie, where you been? We've missed you."

"My human's father died so I've got a lot of sorting out to do," he answered.

"Leave him to it for crying out loud, stop mollycoddling him and leave him to it or he'll never learn. Even if he doesn't do it the state will. They're not going to leave the old man lying around, are they?" Although the response was posed as a question it wasn't one, it was meant as a fact.

By now all of the group had drifted over to him and had heard the reply and thought it hilarious.

Charlie changed the subject. "Where you been, what you been up to?"

The distraction worked and Charlie was told that the group had been to a seance in a house nearby and when the medium had asked for a sign, Z8 had scooped her hair up so that from a distance it looked like it was standing on end. The people who were attending the seance had taken fright and screams and shrieks were heard as some of them fled from the house.

Charlie laughed at the recollection of events although he really didn't think it was funny. He left the group and floated back to his house wondering at the change that had come over him over the last few days. Not too long ago he would have joined in with the rogue shadow group and found what they were doing funny but not now. He wondered if it was because the old man had died or because of the warning he had got from the teacher.

His human was still asleep when he returned so he floated around the house to see what needed doing. He checked the pantry and found that that it was very low on food supplies so, to while away the time, he sat and made a list of essential items that would get them through the next few days. That done he thought about the house and wondered if it would automatically become the property of his human or if his human would be turfed out onto the streets. He began to wish that he had paid more attention to his human as he was growing up and also that he had attended more classes so that he would know what to do, how to cope when things like this happened.

Towards midday he felt his human stirring so quickly attached himself and supported his human washing and dressing before he came downstairs. His human went into the back room and shivered with the chill of it despite it being a sunny day outside. Usually when he came downstairs the fire was roaring away and the room was warm and he had thought nothing of it until now. He stood there looking down at the hearth and wondered how to lay and start a fire, astounded that though he had watched his father do it many times over the years he still had no idea of what to do. He shivered at the thought of his father and gazed at the empty chair for a moment as if visualizing his father still occupying it.

"Dad, dad. Answer me. How do I get this bloody fire sorted out?"

He continued staring towards the empty chair as if expecting an answer, then, after a while he sighed heavily and sloped into the kitchen to see what he could have for breakfast. He found that the cupboard was virtually bare. *Sod it*, he thought as he shoved the last two pieces of stale bread into the toaster and searched around for something to put on them but when he found nothing he ate the toast as it was, washing it down his throat with a cup of black tea as the milk had gone off. He had held the bottle of milk up to his nose hopeful that he would be able to use it and had grimaced comically as the sour smell assailed his nostrils. He then noticed the pile of dishes in the sink. He didn't like washing dishes so had never done it before, he had simply left it all to his father to do, after all the old sod had nothing else to do! Now that all the plates and crockery were used, he had to at least wash a plate and a mug up so that they would be ready for him the next time he was hungry or thirsty. He was surprised and pleased at his forward thinking.

His father had always called him a lazy good for nothing and he had to admit that he was though he always found an excuse for being so and blamed other people for his situation. He didn't blame his mother though although she was one of the reasons he was so lazy. His mother had done everything for him up until she died and wouldn't hear a word against him telling everyone who listened that her son was different to other boys. She saw other boys as being rough and ready but her son was different, he was interested in flowers and trees and nature in general.

A few hours later, Charlie's human was in the supermarket trying to remember what he wanted from the vast array of produce displayed in front of him. He remembered seeing a list for shopping at home though he didn't remember writing it and he also didn't remember to bring it with him. He decided to get essentials for now but couldn't make up his mind what essentials were and wished with all his heart he was somewhere else, preferably in the pub. He had never had to do the shopping as his father had a weekly order delivered and he had got so used to it that he never gave it any thought, that is until now. He didn't want to get too much in as he supposed that the delivery, scheduled two days from now, would still go ahead after all they didn't know that his dad was dead.

Bread, that was it, bread then he could have toast and marmalade so that he could spread it on his toast, what else did he need. He stood staring at the shelves continually getting bumped into by other irritated customers who thought that he was in the way and finally came out of the shop with just bread and marmalade. Once outside the shop he took a deep breath and started towards home. He knew that he hadn't got everything he needed but he felt exhausted, the new experience sapping his energy. Charlie had worked very hard to keep his human focused on getting the shopping but gained small satisfaction from the items purchased. He had conjured up the image of milk and spread in his human's mind but to no avail. Charlie was surprised that humans were such hard work!

Thoroughly distracted, Charlie went over and over the shopping experience and didn't notice that his human had gone into a pub and was downing his second double shot of whisky. Once he noticed he tried to motivate his human to leave but was unsuccessful as a third drink was ordered. His human settled with some of his associates in the pub and they drank as if they all had hollow legs. Charlie spent his time talking to the shadows of the other humans and to his surprise found a lot of disparity in the care they gave their humans. Some were like he had been and couldn't care less that their humans were on a downward spiral but some seemed to really care even though their human overrode them.

Chucking out time found his human loudly shouting his goodbyes and singing tunelessly as he weaved down the street leaving his hard-won shopping on the floor next to where he had been sitting.

How he got home was all due down to Charlie. It took his human quite a while to find which pocket his keys were in, talking loudly to himself as he did so, "They are not in there so they must be in there, nope, well they must be—"and then even longer to try and fit the key in the lock which just wouldn't stay still for him. Charlie didn't have such problems of getting into the house though as shadows could pass through any solid object but he held his irritation and finally got his human inside to collapse in the armchair in which his dad had died.

Charlie detached himself from his human and stood looking down at him for a moment then covered him up and left for his classes. Although he had spent quite a bit of time chatting to the other shadows in the pub none of them knew what procedures to follow when someone died and only one of them offered the suggestion of calling in to the offices to talk to the undertakers. When Charlie told them that they might become shadows to inanimate objects they had simply laughed at him and told him he was sad. They said that shadows had a right to be independent and not be at the beck and call of humans all the time.

Charlie stood looking at a message board trying to decide which lecture to attend, he couldn't find one about when the human they were attached to died so wrote a message on the board asking for such a class to be held then looked through at the various options. He saw one labelled 'inferior/superior' that intrigued him and decided to go to that one although it had already started.

His class was packed but he did manage to squeeze into a space then tuned in to what the teacher was saying, "—astonishing as it may be, nevertheless we must be on our guard against falling in to the same trap. Shadows are not equal to humans, they are here to serve them, to help them reach the highest potential that they can. Can you begin to imagine what chaos would be caused if shadows that were serving our prime minister or members of parliament for example decided that they were better than their human, if they decided that their human were only where they were because of them."

Several hands went up amongst the students and the teacher selected one who asked, "Isn't it true that the people in power only got where they were because of their shadows?"

A murmur of agreement rose and several more hands went up to be waived down by the teacher who then waited for the class to quieten then responded, "All humans have great potential, and it is the shadow's job to nurture that potential. Some shadows are selected to be in the S.A.S. and P.A.T.H. squads and some to look after humans that have power, it is specialised work and they are kept separate. Other shadows, the rest of us, will not initially know what their human is capable of but it should be their sole mission to find out throughout the human's life and help them achieve their potential."

"Is it true that the S.A.S. and the P.A.T.H. squad don't have humans?"

"Yes, although I am not here to talk about them."

The teacher was interrupted again as another murmur of dissent went up. Charlie put his hand up and was surprised to be chosen to speak. "You have very neatly side tracked the initial question you were asked. Will you please answer it?"

The teacher again waited for the class to quieten then said, "It is vitally important to know that, as shadows you are, so to speak, in a position of power. Humans in general don't take too much notice of their shadows and have no idea of the influences that the shadows wield over them whereas you, as shadows know of the power you have." The teacher stopped speaking for a while as she glanced around then said, "To answer your question, yes, the answer is yes and no. People in power mainly get into positions of power because of the diligence of the shadows assigned to them but the humans must also have the ability to handle the power. There is no time to discuss this at the moment, it has a depth that we cannot go into now.

We need to get back on track to examine why some shadows think they are better than the humans they serve."

Charlie had had enough and faded from the group to find a place where he could get his thoughts in order. He found it very confusing that when questions were answered more questions were thrown up. He thought that his teachers were like human politicians who deftly avoided answering anything and planted red herrings deliberately to thwart shadows and divert their attention.

Charlie realised after a time that he had faded from the class because what was being talked about hit home. He was guilty, he had to admit, of thinking that he was better than his human whom he had always thought of as a waste of space and not worthy of his efforts to promote opportunities for him. Charlie wondered why he felt like that and realised that because his human's mother had done so much for him in the beginning, he hadn't had to do anything and he had simply drifted off and done his own thing and let the mother get on with it. True he had had many one-sided discussions with the mother's shadow who kept warning him about his state of inaction but he had simply ignored her and faded away when she tried to talk to him much to her annoyance. He tried to remember her shadow name and had to chase whisps of thought around his head before he remembered that 37 had told him it was B4U.

It had been a major shock to him when the human mother died but by then he was so used to doing nothing that he continued to do it. In the art of doing nothing he was an expert, he thought ruefully. He had had a golden opportunity to learn about how death affected humans but he hadn't remained there to learn about it. He had simply led a riotous life with some fellow shadows and had thought of himself at the time as a real 'Jack the lad'.

Charlie didn't like the thoughts he was having though he knew them to be true. He had left a bereaved child to get on with his life without giving him a thought other than the child wasn't worth his effort and, to be truthful, he had felt himself to be superior to his human.

It was around five o'clock in the morning when Charlie returned to his human and found him still fast asleep in the armchair where he had left him. He carefully studied his human's face and for the first time realised that signs of age were creeping in. His once wavy black hair was flecked with grey around the temples and the relaxed face was full of laughter lines though why they were called laughter lines Charlie had no idea as he had never seen his human laugh.

Charlie busied himself with cleaning out the grate and laying a new fire as he thought through what needed to be done. He decided to live one day at a time as the magnitude of what he had to do threatened to overwhelm him. Today he would steer his human down the road to the undertakers and sort out the funeral arrangements. Tomorrow was another day and he needed not to think about it or to dwell on past issues as it wasn't helpful, he had to try to be in the moment.

Chapter 3 — Animal shadow!

Charlie saw movement out of the corner of his eye and thought for a moment that one of the neighbours had come in because he had left the front door open.

He turned and was surprised to see 37 standing nearby grinning from ear to ear. "Hello," he said.

Charlie was really pleased to see him but was, at the same time, surprised by the visit.

"Hello, 37, nice to see you," he said. "What brings you this way?"

"Guess what, I've passed all of my assessments," said 37.

"All of them, how many did you have for goodness' sake?"

"Five altogether. I was really nervous and thought that I'd mucked up but I passed, I'm still in shock."

"Well, I'm really pleased for you," Charlie said, and he genuinely was but couldn't help asking, "what sort of questions did they ask?"

"Even if I could remember I am not supposed to tell you," 37 responded then, on seeing Charlie's worried expression said, "I went into the truth bubbles each time and all I can remember is being nervous and turning to step in then feeling glad as I was stepping out."

Charlie was quiet for a while then said, "There's something funny about those truth bubbles, don't you think?"

"Yes. Yes, I do. I wonder sometimes at their purpose, I mean they must be there for a reason, don't you think? All the questions I was asked were thrown at me when I was standing outside of them. Don't you think that's strange?"

Both shadows were quiet for a while then Charlie asked, "If you were them (whoever they are), what questions would you ask?"

"I'd ask what they thought the difference was in being a shadow to an animal or a shadow to a human. I would want to know how they thought they could look after such a pure being as an animal when they were a mere shadow. I'd ask about what they thought being selfless was when it was applied to an animal and when it was applied to a human or if they thought it was the same thing for both species."

Charlie's eyes widened knowing that if he had been asked those questions, he wouldn't have been able to give a clear answer. He was quiet for a moment then said, "Well anyway, congratulations, so what does this mean for you, are you going to become a human in your next life?"

"Oh no, nothing like that. I was expecting the assessment board to say that I wasn't good enough yet and to be assigned to shadow another human."

Charlie was surprised. "So, if you think that you are not ready to become a human what did the assessors say when you said that?"

"I didn't tell them."

"You didn't tell them!"

"No."

Charlie realised that he was no nearer to finding out about the next stage in 37's development even though they had spent the last ten minutes talking. "So come on, tell me, the suspense is killing me."

"I'm going to become the shadow of a bird which means that I will spend a lot of time flying. I will be able to travel to lots of places and see life from a different perspective. I will be able to soar high in the sky or close to the sea."

Charlie was dumbstruck, whatever he had been expecting 37 to say it certainly wasn't this.

37 saw the look on Charlie's face and said, "I know, it's brilliant isn't it. The assessment board looked so fierce before I went into the truth bubble. They just kept throwing questions at me sometimes even before I had answered the one before. They gave me the indication each time I came out that I wasn't good enough and I was sure I had failed when suddenly they were all smiles." 37 paused for

breath before continuing with, "They asked me which animal I would like to shadow and I just sat there staring at them whilst trying to take in what they had said."

Charlie was awestruck, he'd never heard of any shadow assigned to an animal never mind meeting someone who was about to be. He looked closely at 37 to see if he was pulling the wool over his eyes but could see no trace of guile.

37 continued, "They were incredibly patient and kind and asked me again which animal I would like to shadow and for a moment I was tempted to say a lion, for who couldn't be in awe in the presence of such a wonderful animal but I heard myself asking if I could be a shadow to a bird."

"No," said Charlie. "A bird! You really asked to be a shadow to a bird!"

"Oh yes," said 37. "I asked if I could be a shadow to a bird, and when asked which one I said albatross. They are truly magnificent. They have such an enormous wingspan which helps them glide over the sea. I've never seen the sea and now I have a chance to, isn't that something!"

"I thought that the next progression from being a shadow was to become a human," said Charlie.

37 responded "You're right, it usually is but the assessors decided to fast track me."

"Not being funny but why you, why did they fast track you, I mean you're nice and all that but why you?"

"Search me," said 37. "When they were firing questions some of them were about animals and I must have said the right thing."

"Tell me what you said again," prompted Charlie thinking that he could store the information away for a later date but he was disappointed as 37 couldn't remember. He said that he thought that animals were here to help humans to realise their potential, to help raise their conscience to another level.

Charlie was astounded. "What? Really, animals are here to help humans and not the other way around?"

"Yes, yes. It's such an honour to be chosen, I'm so excited, see you around sometime," and with that 37 disappeared leaving a very thoughtful Charlie.

Later that day, Charlie's human was feeling very pleased with himself. He had managed to walk past the pub and instead had gone on to the local undertakers where he had everything clearly explained to him and he had signed an agreement for them to take care of his father's funeral. It was amazing how simple it all was really, they did everything, well, nearly everything. All he had to do now was to put an advertisement in the local newspaper, decide what songs he wanted at the service and what wording he wanted on the tombstone, where he was going to hold the reception if he chose to have one and finally, the most important, pay for it all. He had been surprised to learn that they had a family plot in which his father would be interred next to his mother and that there was room for him as well. He had felt brave enough to tell the undertaker that he thought he was dead lucky half expecting him to smile at his wit but the undertaker had heard it all before and gave no reaction whatsoever.

Charlie had worked hard to keep his human on track although every now and then he found himself distracted as he thought about 37. There always had been vague rumours amongst the shadows that some of the high achievers might eventually be chosen to be the shadows of animals and birds but he hadn't really given any credence to it until now and now he couldn't stop thinking about it.

Whilst Charlie was distracted, his human went into the pub and had a couple of beers before Charlie managed to get him to leave it and go to the chippie for a large bag of piping hot chips with loads of salt and vinegar as a treat for doing so well earlier in the day. On arriving home he sat down at the dining table with a sheet of paper in front of him and thought about the wording to put in the newspaper. He wrote, 'It is with the deepest sadness that I have to announce the demise of Cecil Albert Higgins' then put down the pencil and burst into tears.

Charlie eventually managed to get his human settled in bed for the night and left for his classes once he was sure his human was settled. He checked the bulletin board to see if there were any seminars about becoming a shadow to animals but there wasn't a sign of one. He was disappointed, how could he work towards being a shadow to an animal if he couldn't learn how to go about it! He thought of 37 and of his surprise at being chosen and realised that he hadn't been to classes with regard to animals, he hadn't been taught anything different to what Charlie had been taught. How did 37 know what to say!

Charlie found a class discussing humans who have pets and listened intently. He knew that pets were different to wild animals as such but as his human had never expressed any interest in having an animal in the house, he had never bothered. He suddenly stopped this chain of thought; he was excusing himself and that simply wasn't good enough. If he was to become a shadow to an animal, he had to face the truth and the truth was that it had never occurred to him that his human might find joy if an animal chose to live with him, for no matter what a human may wish, if an animal decided that they didn't want to live with a human then they didn't. Charlie found this incredible and couldn't fully understand why animals had this option. He had learnt or had heard it somewhere that animals had never used the option, so he wondered why it was still in place for them. As far as he knew shadows to humans didn't have that option at least none of the shadows he knew had ever mentioned it. Shadows couldn't pick or choose which humans they were to be attached to as far as he knew, they were assigned a human and that was that.

Charlie was engrossed but all too soon the class ended to be continued the following night. Charlie was briefly tempted not to return to his human and see if he could find a day seminar but he felt his human stirring and reluctantly returned and reattached himself to him.

Charlie hadn't previously realised how lucky he was with his human being born into a wealthy family and he had just taken all the trimmings that came with wealth for granted. Now, as his human sat in the bank with the manager, he looked around himself and noticed that nobody was smiling, nobody looked happy. Charlie pulled himself back into the moment and finished the solemn business of steering his human into dealing with his father's considerable assets.

Charlie's human felt really satisfied with himself at what he was achieving and felt that maybe for the first time in his life his father would have been proud of him. How ironic, he thought, that his father had to die before he could show him that his one and only child wasn't a good for nothing! He suddenly felt the urge to look around and, for the first time noticed that not one of the people he could see looked happy. So stuck in his own private world of blaming his father and drinking himself into a stupor he hadn't noticed what was going on around him. He tipped his hat at the bank manager and warmly thanked him for his services then left the bank and walked homeward although he could easily have ordered a cab. His father was incredibly rich but frugal. He had not believed in wasting money on trappings of any sort, they had a roof over their heads and for that they should be thankful.

The house they lived in echoed these sentiments with the basics of furniture. Charlie's human looked around himself and realised how drab the house had become, he had been living in it all these years and suddenly his eyes were opened, and he saw the reality, no wonder he sometimes felt depressed. He wondered when the purple wallpaper had been put up surprised that it could ever have been in fashion, that someone had actually chosen it and had loved it so much that it was plastered throughout the entire house. It was puce in more ways than one! The thought came into his mind that it must have been a job lot and he surprised himself by smiling.

Later that afternoon, Charlie's human found himself in a huge DIY department store totally confused by the vast array of displays. He couldn't make his mind up on which colour to have and then, when he did, he then decided against painting the walls having seen wallpaper he liked. He imagined the wallpaper in his front room after he had put it up, after all, he reasoned, it shouldn't be too difficult, any fool could do it. He held that thought of doing the decorating himself until he looked at the vast array of equipment needed, brushes for painting skirting boards (he didn't know what they were) as well as brushes for pasting, tins of paint, white spirit, tape measures, plum lines, scissors, a trestle table, the list went on and on. He was overwhelmed and decided there and then that decorating needed an expert to do it. He asked one of the workers in the shop how he could find someone to do the work and was directed to a cork notice board with a myriad of cards offering various services pinned on to it.

Charlie was getting fed up and his human was beginning to get a headache, so he encouraged his human to take the first card he saw from the board. He was told to put it back and simply copy the number down by a member of staff. Charlie's human was all for throwing a strop and marching out of the shop but somehow, he managed to hold himself together and copied the name and number down on a scrap of paper with a borrowed pen and made his way home calling in to the local chippie for cod and chips and mushy peas.

It wasn't until he reached home that he realised that the phone number was of no use to him as his phone had been cut off because he hadn't paid the phone bill. He had rarely used it as his father had called phones a waste of time and money so it just sat there in the hall, gathering dust. That it was there at all was a reluctant concession on his father's part as he gave into his wife's request that they should have one if ever there was an emergency.

Charlie's human wondered if there had been address on the business card but in his haste to copy the number down, he hadn't noticed it. Sod it, he thought, he would now have to go out and use one of the red public phone boxes. He sat down to eat his fish and chips out of the paper feeling a rebel as he did so, in fact he actually giggled at the picture in his mind of the consternation on his father's face when he thought standards were being dropped. He noticed that the fire had been prepared for lighting though he couldn't remember preparing it and once he had got it going, with plenty of use of the bellows and firelighters, he sat and watched the flickering flames and soon was lulled into a deep sleep.

Charlie separated himself from his human, glad to have some downtime for himself. He knew he shouldn't but he reckoned on having an hour or so before his human woke so he would have plenty of time to get his jumbled thoughts sorted out. Since talking to 37 his mind had been in a whirl, he had never talked with anyone who was offered the choice of an animal or a bird before and he wanted it so much for himself. He had to admit to himself that he was jealous of 37, he wanted to change places with 37 without all the hard work that 37 had put in and yes, he had to admit, 37 had been diligent and had only detached himself from his human to go to classes and had worked hard for his human to have opportunities for inner growth whilst Charlie had simply despised his human, ignored his offers of help and had left his human to get on with life without helping him in any way.

At the time hanging out with the other rogue shadows had seemed like the fun thing to do but now he realised he had simply blotted his copy book and that his aspirations of becoming a shadow to an animal or bird would always remain an unfulfilled dream in his mind unless he really went to town and turned things around. He consoled himself with the thought that at least he had started to turn things around but wondered if it was too little too late. If his human died tomorrow, for example, he would fail miserably and he had no doubt that he would be doomed to be a shadow to a statue or a lamp post or something. The thought that his human could die tomorrow or anytime soon alarmed him and he wished, for a brief moment that he was out partying with the rogue shadows completely ignorant of the downward spiral he had been in.

All too soon his human started to waken and Charlie quickly reattached himself realising that he had made little or no progress in sorting his thoughts out. Charlie's human, on the other hand seemed rather pleased with his efforts throughout the day. That evening he banked up the fire, checked around the house and went up to bed and soon was fast asleep again.

Charlie floated away to attend a seminar and was surprised when a voice from the past spoke to him.

"Hello Charlie, where you been lately?"

Charlie looked around and saw one of his mates from the rogue shadows gang standing nearby.

"What you doing here?" he asked, genuinely surprised to see him.

"4Z9 got downgraded to shadow a statue and everyone has suddenly woken up to the fact that it could happen to them as well. I don't know how long the effect of what happened to him will last, I mean, it's happened before loads of times and the gang has always got back together but this time it seems different, I mean 4Z9 was pretty popular as our leader and we all thought he was untouchable."

Charlie was astonished, 4Z9 had been his hero, he couldn't imagine that his vibrant personality could be subdued in such a way. A thought occurred to him. "Which statue?"

"Winston Churchill in Woodford Green."

"Oh. Well at least he's a shadow to a statue of someone who was famous, that must count for something."

His mate floated away and Charlie struggled to remember his name but, in the end, gave up and checked the notice board for what seminars were taking place and soon found himself listening to one about 'respect for the human we shadow'. Once upon a time he would have avoided such seminars like the plague but now he found that he was actually enjoying it and was learning something from it. He hadn't realised that humans were so complex, he had judged them all by his previous experience of being a human and his thirty-seven years this time around of being a shadow, as being shallow and weak and easy to manipulate but this was far from the truth. It was unwise to think that all humans were the same and responded to certain stimulus the same, they were a motley crew. A blanket statement would never do, that was for sure. Different experiences moulded them and either tainted or enriched their lives.

At the end of the seminar, Charlie took himself away from the other shadows and assimilated what he had heard. The seminar he had just listened to was the first of six on the same subject and he wondered if he could absorb all the information.

He thought about his human and to his surprise found that although he didn't respect him, yet he was beginning to like him. It wasn't enough though it was a start. These things couldn't be rushed. He could say that he respected his human but it wouldn't be the truth, the words would be hollow. He began to wish that he hadn't wasted so much time mixing with the rogue shadows when his human was younger and instead had spent more time supporting and gently guiding him. *That was it*, he thought, *gentle guidance*. He could not go at the relationship like a bull at a gate, it took time, effort and sincerity amongst other things. Like a puppet master, he had to learn how to control and sometimes manipulate his human as they both discovered his human's personality, skills and other traits that might be developed along the way.

Charlie returned to his human and reattached himself and his human went through the morning ablutions before going downstairs to breakfast. As he reached the bottom stair, there was a knock on the door and he opened it to find a supermarket delivery man. *Great*, he thought, *thank goodness I don't have to go out shopping any more.* He unpacked the carrier bags and shoved the contents anywhere that there was space in the walk-in larder, then made himself breakfast.

Once he had had his breakfast, he thought about what he was going to do and realised that the first thing was to find some change so that he would be able to use the telephone down the road to ring up the painter and decorator, it never occurred to him to negate the problem by simply paying the phone bill!

After he had made himself yet another cup of tea he searched through his coat and trouser pockets for change, then, when he couldn't find much, he thrust his hands down the sides of the armchair and the back of the sofa and found what he thought was more than enough although he had no idea how much a call would cost him. He looked through the money he had collected and found he had quite a few foreign coins and wondered if the machine in the telephone box would accept them then thrust them all in his pocket thinking that he would soon find out one way or another.

Charlie put a thought in his human's mind to decide which room to decorate first for although the whole house needed doing it would be prudent, he surmised, to have just the one room done first so he could judge the quality of the workmanship. Charlie's human was pleased with how he was thinking and strode through the downstairs rooms to pick a room to decorate. He found it very difficult at first but eventually decided that the front room would be the one to have a facelift. He stood in the middle of the room, hands on his hips, and looked around himself and suddenly saw what a drab room it was. The piles of dust and hanging cobwebs didn't add any charisma at all, there was no doubt about it, he would have to clean it thoroughly first after all he couldn't have a stranger coming in to decorate his house and see what a state it was in.

Charlie's human eventually found a feather duster and started tackling the cobwebs grimacing with distaste as he did so. Once done he found an old stepladder that he never knew he had in the garden shed that he never went into and set them up in the front room, got himself a bucket of hot soapy water and proceeded to wash the walls down. Once he had finished cleaning one wall, he had his elevenses then continued washing down the other walls. It was early evening when he finished and he was too tired to do anything else. He would clean the windows, do the dusting and wash the net curtains tomorrow. No wonder his mother had died young, he had never realised that housework was such hard work! He grabbed a quick sandwich then took himself upstairs and had a shower obviously well pleased with himself as he sang tunelessly at the top of his voice before going to bed. Eating just before going to bed was not such a good idea and Charlie found that his human was extremely restless for some time.

Once he was sure that his human had settled down for the night Charlie detached himself and floated over to the Churchill statue in Woodford Green to say hello to 4Z9 before continuing to his class to catch the second part of his seminar. 4Z9 was in a sorry state and was nothing like the gang ring leader he used to be and Charlie felt really sad for him and promised to return for more visits. As he moved away, he knew that his determination to do his best for his human from now on was strongly reinforced, there was no way, no way that he was going to end up a shadow to a still object!

The second seminar opened up new challenges for him as he struggled to overcome the thought that he might not succeed, that he might fail his human. Charlie had never even thought of the possibility of failing in anything but now the possibility swamped him and he could think of nothing else. For a time he became his own worst enemy.

Chapter 4 — Decorating mayhem

Charlie's human awoke stiff and sore and definitely did not want to get up to face the day but, in the end, his need to use the toilet made him move. He couldn't understand why he still felt so tired, after all, he had had a good twelve hours' sleep. He moaned and grumbled to himself but eventually got dressed and stumbled downstairs to put the kettle on for a nice reviving cup of tea. Whilst waiting for it to boil he found that he had run out of teabags and for a moment this seemed like the greatest catastrophe in the world.

Charlie had to work hard to get his human to make and finish his breakfast and wash up after himself. This was the most his human had ever done for himself in his life up until his father had died and he was finding it hard to get into a routine and obey the little voice in his head that told him to clear up his mess as nobody else was going to.

That done, Charlie's human went into the front room to survey his efforts of the following day and was disappointed that after all his hard work it still looked the same, still looked drab and dreary. He took down the grey net curtains and put them on a cycle in the washing machine, his enthusiasm for finishing cleaning the room rapidly diminishing with every second that slowly ticked by and it took a lot of work from Charlie before his human got a bucket of hot soapy water and a sponge ready to clean the windows and surrounding woodwork. He continued to moan and groan his lot as he washed the windows and wiped off the paintwork but as he saw how good they were beginning to look he became more and more enthusiastic and, after a time, he even began whistling cheerfully. He then put some vinegar and lemon in a bowl and with the aid of some newspaper wiped the windows dry so that they sparkled. The room looked so much brighter and he went into the kitchen in a much better frame of mind to have a midday snack until he remembered that he had no teabags.

On the table in the kitchen was the piece of paper that he had started to write about his dad's funeral. Sod it, he had forgotten to finish it. He grabbed a pen and wrote the time and the place for his dad's funeral, asked for donations to be sent to a local hospice, (he didn't know where this thought had come from but he liked it as he thought it made him look like a caring sort of person), instead of bringing flowers and stuck the piece of paper in an envelope. He didn't know where to send it so decided he would go out later and buy a local paper for the address then he could buy himself some teabags and pop into the post office for some stamps.

After finishing his snack he found a reasonably clean duster and went back into the front room and kicked over the bucket of dirty water that he had left just inside the door which he had used to clean the windows with. He picked up the bucket and threw it across the room accompanied by foul language. The bucket hit one of the walls he had cleaned the previous day and sprayed its remaining contents over it.

It took Charlie quite a time to calm his human down, and in the end, he encouraged his human to leave the house and go shopping. His human remembered to buy the local newspaper, teabags and postage stamps and Charlie began to fall into relax mode until he realised his human had gone into the pub and was downing lager like it was out of fashion all the while griping about how unfair everything was. Charlie couldn't get him out of the pub and the landlord only managed to because it was closing time. As the landlord stood outside the pub watching his customer weave down the road singing bawdy songs and waving his shopping bag about, he shook his head, wiped his hands down his trousers a few times then went back inside the pub and began to lock up.

Charlie didn't go to his class that night as he felt too ashamed that he had let his human down.

Shame was a new feeling for him and he didn't like the feeling of it one bit so as a sort of punishment to himself he remained attached to his human all night as his human snored on the kitchen floor until the early hours. A call of nature prompt stirred his human who managed to stagger into the downstairs toilet and relieve himself. On coming back into the kitchen he picked up a shopping bag and put it on the side then stumbled up the stairs and fell onto his bed almost falling asleep before he landed.

Charlie thought about the seminar he had missed and wondered about the content of it. He detached himself for a while and stretched then looked down at his human thinking how difficult it was to respect someone when you knew every intimate detail about them. He sat pondering this thought until mid-afternoon when he felt his human stirring then quickly reattached himself having decided that whether or not he felt guilty in the future he would not stay attached overnight again, it caused him to worry too much.

Charlie's human was frustrated, he had gone through the paper several times scrutinising every page but was unable to find their address. He threw the paper down on the kitchen top and it fell open on the page where its address was displayed so he quickly copied it down, found a stamp from the book he had purchased from the post office the previous day and walked out to the nearest post box. As he walked, he noticed several people staring at him and he thumbed his nose at them before Charlie could stop him, posted his letter and walked back home. He caught sight of himself in the hall mirror as he entered the house and for a moment didn't recognise himself. He was looking unkempt to say the least and was still wearing yesterday's clothes.

After a shower and a change of clothes he was feeling much better about himself although he had a blinding headache. Once downstairs, he looked into the front room and saw the mess he had left the previous day. The carpet near the door was saturated, and he spend a long time placing towels on it and walking over them to absorb the moisture. When he went to put the towels in the washing machine, he found the net curtains he had forgotten to take out of the machine. He dropped his wet bundle of towels on the floor, wiped his palms down his jumper then took the nets out into the garden to hang on the rotary drier. The nets were nothing like what he had put into the machine, they were white and really quite pretty.

Later that evening, he was beginning to feel much better and after he had made himself a cup of tea and some cheese on toast, he settled down to watch the box. When the programme finished, he got up and stretched, turned the box off then looked out of the back window to see his net curtains whizzing merrily around in the strong wind. He opened the back door to fetch them in then realised that it was pouring with rain so quickly shut the back door thinking it was no use getting the nets in as they would be wetter than when he hung them out!

He shivered as he shut the kitchen door and thought thank goodness that he didn't have a dog as going out for a walk in this weather would be unpleasant to say the least. This thought had not been prompted by Charlie who suddenly came to attention with a jolt causing his human to stop and stare blankly at nothing for a few moments. When Charlie realised what had happened, he quickly brought his human back into the moment and aided him with his bedtime routine.

Once his human was settled, Charlie went downstairs and hovered in the front room surveying the mess. He mused over the random thought his human had had and thought that getting a dog, or a cat for that matter would mean that he would be sharing the house with an animal shadow. He was quite excited by the idea and couldn't believe that his human had thought of it all by himself!

He made his way to his class and found a teacher who was giving the seminar he had missed but, although it was interesting it was hard to keep his mind on track, distracted as he was by the possibility of sharing his house with an animal shadow!

Chapter 5 — 4Z9

Early the following morning Charlie's human was walking through the local shopping centre when he noticed a mobile phone shop and without hesitation he went in and wandered around the shop having no idea what he was looking for but fascinated by the displays. He soon found himself accosted by a sales assistant who asked him what type of phone he was looking for or did he come in for upgrade information.

Charlie's human had no idea what the assistant was talking about so simply said that he had come in to buy the latest phone for his niece but that he knew nothing about them so would the assistant please explain the similarities and differences.

The sales assistant heard 'latest phone' and nothing else and soon had his customer floundering in the midst of all the information he was being given.

Charlie's human did not want to appear as if he knew nothing at all about mobile phones even though he had told that to the sales assistant but he managed to convey the truth of what he had said quite easily. Charlie could see that the sales assistant was working his human, but he couldn't get his human to see it no matter how hard he tried so in the end had to stay quiet and just watch.

Half an hour later Charlie's human was walking home feeling really pleased with himself and couldn't wait to get back to try out his new possession. Once home he put the kettle on for a cup of tea then briefly looked at the paperwork he had signed then thrust it aside and examined his purchase. He tipped the various bits and pieces out of the box then arranged them all in front of where he was sitting as feelings of uncertainty drifted up into his mind. What on earth were all the bits for? He eventually read the part of the instruction leaflet to identify what each piece was and felt quite pleased with himself when he was able to put the phone on charge. Settling down on the sofa with a cup of tea he then looked through the paperwork managing to confuse himself with the operating instructions.

When the phone was fully charged, he pressed the 'on/off' button on the side a few times happy for a brief time that he didn't now have to route around for change to use in the local telephone box, he could call anyone he liked from home and not only that people could reach him although he knew that if he had paid his phone bill, they would be able to reach him anyway.

The euphoria only lasted a little time as he realised that no one was going to call him on his mobile as they didn't know he had one and anyway even he didn't know his new number and he had just bought the thing! How was he going to be able to get people to phone him on it? He was sure that you didn't advertise the number in the paper to let people know of it so how was he supposed to let people know? He searched through all of the paperwork sure that the sales assistant had written his number down somewhere for him but eventually found it on a card in his jacket pocket when he was looking for something else. He wondered what his dad would say if he had been showed the shiny new phone and for a while wished he hadn't given into temptation and purchased it. His dad would have said it was a waste of money and he would have been right. His dad would have called it a white elephant or something like that! He stopped for a while staring unseeingly into the distance with a half-smile on his face as he thought of all the white elephants that his dad had talked about trying to fit into the house with him.

He had a eureka moment. He could phone the decorator if he could remember where he had put the card. Overwhelmed with all the new technology he fell asleep in the sofa. Charlie detached himself and made himself familiar with the phone so that he could help his human. The phone was far too sophisticated for a first time buy and Charlie wished he had tried harder to get his human to get a cheaper phone with less gadgets. Once he had worked out how to make a call and had found the card from the decorator Charlie reattached himself and began to put seeds of getting a dog from a rescue home in his human's mind.

When Charlie's human awoke, he felt refreshed and ready to take on the world. He picked up the phone surprised to see the DIY card next to it, dialled the number and made arrangements for the person to call round the following afternoon at three o'clock then, put the piece if paper with the mobile number on it back in his pocket after writing it down in his empty address book under 'me' and left the house to call in to the undertaker to inform him of the hymns that he wanted at the service and to leave his new number in exchange for theirs, then went into the bank to leave contact details. When he returned home, he immediately wrote the numbers of the places he had visited in his address book and made himself a substantial dinner to reward himself for joining the human race. He wondered, as he prepared his meal, if everyone who had a mobile phone carried their address book around with them as well in case they wanted to call somebody whilst they were out!

Charlie was late going to the seminar as his human had trouble getting to sleep and he couldn't leave him until he knew he was settled but did, he admitted to himself, become a little impatient and irritated as he waited. He would have to work on these tendencies as they were not helpful and perhaps were the cause of his human being restless! He gave thanks that he could at least have some time away from his human unlike shadows who were assigned to immovable objects. Charlie shivered at the thought of it and vowed to work harder to help his human achieve the best he could. He still didn't feel love for his human but he didn't dislike him either and sometimes his human had done things that had made him laugh though his laughter was not malicious in any way, more of a kindly laughter as when his human had bought a phone but had nobody to ring him until he went out and gave his number to them. The phone in question sat in pride of place in the kitchen sleek and shiny and fully charged.

Charlie joined his seminar midway through and was surprised when the teacher suddenly stopped giving information out and suddenly started asking for it. Unfortunately for him, he was the first one to be chosen to answer the question.

"Why does respect have to be earned, why can't it be freely given?" Charlie thought it unfair that he had been given two questions in one but managed to give a satisfactory answer to turn the attention away from himself and on to someone else. Moments after, he wondered what he had said, how did he answer but for the life of him he couldn't remember. He eventually managed to stop searching his mind and instead listened to some of the answers that other shadows were giving. He was on tenterhooks in case the teacher picked on him again and prepared a ready answer in case she did but he need not have worried as she suddenly stopped asking questions and went back to giving out information instead.

On the way back to his human, Charlie called upon 4Z9 and told him all about his human and the seminar he had attended. He must have sounded fed up, as 4Z9 offered to change places with him. Charlie shook his head but 4Z9 became persistent and in the end, Charlie left him. He was feeling puzzled, was it possible to change places with a shadow of a still object, he didn't think so but he didn't know for sure. He remembered that when he was hanging around with the rogue shadows, they sometimes used to attach themselves to humans whose shadows had left for classes or humans who for some reason or other had lost or had never had a shadow. They used to make the humans do things that they wouldn't normally do and very rarely came up against a human who couldn't be manipulated. He used to have a fine old time but now, as he thought about it, he cringed inside and asked himself the question of why some humans didn't have shadows at all. He couldn't answer the question but decided that when he went for his next seminar, he would ask a teacher if he remembered to.

The following afternoon the decorator called around at three o'clock on the dot and Charlie's human showed him the room and asked him how much it would cost although he had no idea of what jobs like his usually cost. The decorator gave him a price that he thought was reasonable and told him he would have to buy x number of ready pasted wallpaper rolls, one x tin of white emulsion and one x tin of white gloss paint ready for the following Monday morning.

Charlie's human felt ecstatic, he hadn't realised how demanding it would be getting the job done but he had done it, well, not done it exactly as the job hadn't been started yet, but he had got the ball rolling so to speak. He would go out tomorrow and purchase the wallpaper he had liked, after all, it shouldn't be that difficult, should it?

Charlie's human settled himself down in front of the television with a couple of beers and spent a very pleasant late afternoon and evening either dozing or watching film repeats. Charlie liked having a relaxing evening and wanted to spend time thinking about what 4Z9 had said but dare not in case in case he passed on some of his thoughts to his human. He knew he could manipulate his human and help change his mind but was only allowed to do so if his human was set on a path of destruction. He had misused this power before and had thought it hilarious but now he would never do such a thing again. He had been given a chance to change and he was going to take it. What he wasn't sure of was if he quietly had the thoughts to himself whilst his human was gainfully occupied would he leave a residue of them in his human! Deep down Charlie knew the answer to his searching question, knew that whilst he was attached to his human, he could transfer his thought patterns.

Charlie detached himself from his human after checking that he was comfortable and relaxed and focused on the television programme then thought about all the times before when he had been assigned to this particular human and realised that he had been detached from his human more times than he had been attached to him during his thirty-seven years of life and that during those times he had been attached to him he had disliked him intensely and amongst other things had thought of him as a weak insignificant fool.

Charlie was horrified as he realised that when he was attached, he had passed these feelings onto his human, no wonder his human had a poor self-image and low self-worth. Charlie then realised that it wasn't his human's fault at all for being how he was, the painful truth he had to face that it was his fault, he had engendered the behaviour in his adult and in sneering at him he was actually sneering at himself! He had pointed a single figure of spite at his human not realising that the other three fingers on his hand were pointing back at him!

Charlie briefly came out of his intense thoughts just to check that his human was still settled then returned to his thoughts wondering why such thoughts he was now having were so obvious when they became obvious but weren't obvious at all before they were thought of!

Charlie wallowed in the shame of his actions but was pleased that he was not attached to his human to pass them on to him. This, for him was an eureka moment, he had become aware how badly his thoughts could affect his human and he had detached himself so as not to affect him with them, perhaps there was light at the end of the tunnel after all! Charlie reattached himself to his human and concentrated on his well-being as any shadow worth his weightlessness should do having completely forgotten to examine what 4Z9 had said about changing places.

Chapter 6 — New suit

The Sunday prior to when the decorating was due to start, Charlie's human spent most of the day cleaning the downstairs toilet, which, over the years, had become a storehouse for odds and ends as he didn't want the person coming to his house to think badly of him. Although the toilet facility was small, it took him most of the day and he was happy when he finished and had settled down in front of the television for the evening with a large plate of sandwiches at hand.

The week flew by and where initially Charlie's human found it difficult to have a stranger in the house, he soon began to look forward to the little tea breaks. Charlie also enjoyed having another shadow in the house but found that the other shadow wasn't given to small talk as he just concentrated all his efforts in helping his human do a good job. Charlie began to use him as a role model whilst he had the chance.

At last, the job was finished and the DIY person had packed up and finished, leaving Charlie's human standing in the middle of the transformed room. There was something wrong but for a while he couldn't put his finger on it, then it struck him, the drab furniture had been almost camouflaged in the drab front room but now it had nowhere to hide. Nothing for it, he would have to go up the city and find a furniture store and buy new stuff and while he was about it, he had better get the curtains changed, no use doing half a job. He was disappointed that the room wasn't finished, that he hadn't previously thought about the furnishings but decided that he was only human, and humans were allowed to make mistakes as long as they learnt from them. He was surprised and pleased with himself that he could have such profound thoughts, maybe there was hope for him yet.

On his way to his seminar, Charlie called in to see 4Z9 who got straight to the point and asked him if he'd considered changing places as he didn't seem too happy with his human and Charlie told him straight out before he lost his nerve that he didn't want to change. 4Z9 had been the leader of the shadow gang and was very charismatic and able to manipulate other shadows and humans easily. Charlie very nearly hadn't come as he didn't want to fall under his spell again and do something that, with his new awareness, he might later regret. 4Z9 changed his tactics, telling Charlie that the statue he was assigned to was of a very important figure and yes, although he was still the shadow of a still figure it was a lot better than being assigned to a toilet block or a telegraph pole.

Charlie found himself becoming mesmerized and realised that 4Z9 was working him. With a lot of effort he suddenly snapped out of the vagueness and became alert and speedily left for the seminar with 4Z9's laughter ringing in his ears along with the words. "I nearly had you."

Charlie was frightened at how quickly he had succumbed to 4Z9's attempt to change places with him and vowed never to go near him again or at least not go anywhere near him until he was stronger.

Later that night, he examined his fears with a counsellor and although he didn't give out 4Z9's name it was very easy to identify him from what was said.

Charlie asked the counsellor if it was possible for shadows to change places that is, from a still form to a human and was horrified when told that it was possible in rare cases although the changeover wouldn't be for long as it would become evident in the different behaviour of the human they were attached to and the different vibrations that were being sent out. When initially being assigned to a human, each shadow is given a vibration which is logged so a change in the frequency would send out an alert and the Shadow Authenticity Squads would be alerted and vacuum them out of the human and return them to twenty-four-seven schooling programmes or in some cases transfer them into a holding container until they were reassessed, classified and reassigned to a new human. They could only finish the schooling with a pass mark of 100% and were often reassigned to a statue for maybe a thousand years or more until they achieved full marks.

Charlie then had a heart-to-heart with the counsellor as he confided all his previous misdemeanours although everything he said was already known and on his record. The counsellor was, however, aware that Charlie was trying to change and become a better shadow to his human but couldn't pass this information on to Charlie. Charlie should be guided by his inner feelings for that was the only way forward for him or anyone. His pathway wasn't going to be made easier because he had had a change of mind, for he would at times be tested almost beyond his limit. He could either put up or shut up, give out or give in.

Charlie realised what a narrow escape he had had both in nearly allowing himself to be trapped by 4Z9 and in wasting more than thirty years of his human's life whilst he did his own thing. He didn't feel angry at 4Z9 though, he just felt rather sad for him and prayed that he would turn his behaviour around.

Charlie's human was feeling rather proud of himself and he whistled at the top of his voice half expecting his father to tell him to shut up. The thought of his father sobered him up for a little while but he soon was back to whistling the same song over and over again.

Mid-morning he was strolling along the High Street and picked up a local paper to read on the train into town. He thought about his newly decorated room and pictured the whole house being redecorated but first thing's first, he had to get the furniture for his front room. As he stood on the platform, he wondered what would happen to the old furniture, wondered if the firm he was going to get his new furniture from would take it away or not. The thought worried him for a while but soon he was sitting in the train on a seat by the window and staring out the surrounding countryside surprised that there seemed to be so much countryside left. After a while he started to read through his paper and found the piece he had put in the paper advising of the coming service. That brought him up with a jolt, he had been so busy thinking about decorating his house that he had not given his father a thought, mind you, he thought uncharitably, his father hadn't thought much about him either.

Charlie didn't like how his human was thinking and worked hard trying to get his human to forgive and move on and succeeded in making his human feel a little guilty though not for long.

Charlie's human, with a lot of interaction by Charlie, finally bought himself a modern three-piece suite, a coffee table (although he only drank tea) and a rather magnificent bookcase. He didn't have any books to put in it but that was a moot point, he liked it, so he was getting it and that was that.

He called into a public house to have meal and a pint noticing the smartly dressed city workers who were also eating and drinking. He wondered if he put on a suit like they wore if he would be able to blend in so that he would be thought of as one of them. Something was niggling him and though he tried to chase the thought he couldn't quite catch it, what on earth was the matter.

He was making his way back to the station when he had it, suits, what was troubling him was the suits he kept seeing. He needed a suit for his dad's funeral which was in the following week. Suddenly he didn't feel so cheerful or clever, he had left it far too late to have a suit made so he would just have to make the best of it and either buy one off of the peg or make do with the dowdy suits he already had in his wardrobe. He grimaced, there was no way he was going to wear any of the suits in his wardrobe, he should have outed them yonks ago and anyway, if he remembered rightly, they were all grey and nobody wore grey to a funeral these days, did they!

He finally bought a smart dark blue pinstriped suit although he didn't like it very much as he thought it made him look fat then realised he was making a lot of fuss about nothing in particular as he only aimed to wear it the once.

Whilst his human was trying on different styles, Charlie chatted to the shadow of the salesperson who was helping him choose and found that his human was the proud keeper of a dog. Charlie listened intently as RS2 told him of the conversations and experiences he had had with the dog's shadow and Charlie wished with all his heart that his human had a dog. He told RS2 he would look out for him in the seminars then left the store with his human not fully engaged with what his human was doing as his mind was focused on how to get his human to buy a dog. He was going to plant seeds in his humans mind ages ago after his conversation with 37 and couldn't understand why he hadn't done so.

Charlie's human ambled along the road to the station and managed to get on the right platform and board the right train by himself. Charlie realised that he had been so busy with his thoughts that he had briefly left his human to fend for himself and in so doing had made him vulnerable so quickly focused fully on him and got him home safely. Charlie was frustrated with himself but couldn't dwell on the fact whilst he was still attached because of the negative effect it would have on his human, all sorts of things could happen and he just didn't want to take the chance of anything happening for then he would put the privilege of being a shadow to an animal totally out of reach.

Chapter 7 — Daffodils

"Listen everybody, it's very important that you listen, really listen, your task is all about responsibility. From the word 'go' you are put in sole charge of your human twenty-four-seven. What sort of life they have is, in the main, entirely dependent on you. In some very rare cases the human is stronger than the shadow and will not listen but if a downward spiral is in evidence the shadow should never ever give up or give in, should never stop believing that a difference can be made."

Many of the shadows put their hands up to ask questions but were ignored as the teacher continued, "Up until the last millisecond of life it is possible to promote positive change in any human, I know, I have done it myself. Remember the darkest hour is just before the dawn."

Again a show of hands went up and this time the teacher selected one. "What if the human doesn't change, will the shadow be demoted to still life shadowing because of it?"

All the hands went down and silence ensued as every shadow present focused on the teacher who smiled then said, "At last I have your full attention" then paused for a moment causing some shadows to become impatient then continued by saying, "It depends on whether the shadow has worked twenty-four-seven with the human. I know of shadows who, once attached at the birth of their human stayed attached throughout the life of the human until they died."

There was stunned silence. Charlie searched his memory but couldn't remember any of the shadows that he had come in contact with remaining attached throughout the life of their human. 37 was the only shadow he knew who came anywhere near what the teacher had described for he knew that 37 had truly loved his human all of his life.

The teacher continued, "You may or may not be impressed with what I have just said but you need to know that just because a shadow remains attached twenty-four-seven doesn't mean that they are diligent or should be admired. For one thing they don't attend seminars so have no way of knowing that what they are doing is correct or if there is a better way to assist their human by updating their thinking."

Charlie had to admit that he had begun to doubt himself but was heartened by what the teacher had said. He still felt guilty at wasting so much of his human's life but was determined that he would try his hardest from now on so that even if he didn't succeed at least he had tried to turn things around.

He realised he was nightdreaming and tuned in to the teacher. "About 1% of shadows have a reason to stay attached to their humans but at the moment monitoring has found that 9% of shadows are doing so. This is a concern and work is continuing to jolt the shadows who are behaving in a comatose fashion to come out of it."

The seminar gave Charlie a lot to think about, he hadn't intended to attend it as he had wanted the finish the six-part course he had started on. He realised that even though the teacher had answered many questions she had raised many more. The teacher had spoken about shadows who were attached to their humans all of the time but hadn't broached the subject of shadows who were rarely if ever attached though he thought that perhaps he might not be as attentive if such a seminar came up as he would think that it was being aimed at him. He wondered how long he had to try to make amends, he knew that a human could be 'saved' right up until the last millisecond of his life if he asked to be but he didn't think the same thing applied to shadows as shadows couldn't die. Charlie wondered if he could make up for lost time and wished he could know how long his human had to live so that he could plan accordingly after all, he reasoned, if his human was going to die next week he might just as well give up now.

The fact that he thought his human could die next week or sometime soon connected him with the memory that his human's father was going to be buried the following week so he had to at least wait until after then before his human found joy and meaning in his life, after all, society certainly would frown on him if he went about enjoying himself whilst his father lay in the mortuary!

Charlie's human came downstairs full of purpose, whilst lying in bed thinking about how the new furniture would look, he suddenly realised that he had not thought about getting a new carpet in the front room. The carpet in there was old even before he arrived at the scene and he thought that perhaps the frugal nature of his father meant that it stayed not that he was complaining of course, the very fact that he had so much money to spend was because his father had spent so little of it in his lifetime.

In the kitchen after breakfast he noticed that the word 'message' was flashing on his phone and got really excited but in his eagerness to see it he managed to delete it and then spent quite a long time worrying who it was and whether the message was important or not. He thought about taking his phone back to the shop from which he had purchased it ask them if they could recover it then realised that he couldn't do that as he had said he was buying the phone for his niece and he didn't want to be caught out in a blatant lie.

Charlie encouraged his human to go out to the carpet shop and chose a thick pile carpet plus underlay then arrange for a fitter to call around the following day to take proper measurements as he only had his mother's tape measure from when she used to sew and that was by no means big enough and anyway, he wasn't sure where it was. Once done and feeling mighty pleased with himself, he then called into the local pub for a dinner and a nice cold pint. Whilst he was eating, he wondered if there was anything else he needed to do before his father's funeral and realised that he hadn't composed a speech or organised a reception. He decided then and there to not have a reception and began to scribble down notes, with a pen he had borrowed from the bar, on the sides of a local newspaper he had just purchased about how he loved and missed his father then scribbled it out as it was obviously untrue and people, if any attended the service, would know him to be a liar and he couldn't have that. He was proud of his name if not his father and would not have it blemished in any way.

On the way home he called into the local park and sat on a bench people watching and as he relaxed childhood memories came flooding back and he remembered that his father had loved a poem about daffodils and had often recited it to his family making them sit down to listen to him. His father, he realised, had been a bit of a showman in his younger days as he walked up and down the front room waving his hands about and pulling faces. His mother and he would fall about laughing and loudly clap him when he finished reciting and bowed to them, his audience. Funny, he had completely forgotten about those times and a single tear spilled over from one of his eyes down onto his cheek and rolled down his face leaving a wet trail behind it. He wished with all of his heart that he could go back to those times and experience them all over again but he knew he couldn't as the time had been spent. Funny thing about time, more precious than money but in some cases spent the same way, it could be so easily wasted and thrown away on some frivolity or other.

Feeling philosophical he wandered home feeling kindlier towards his father than he had in years. As he strolled home, he decided that he would recite the poem at his dad's funeral if he could just remember how it went.

The following day the carpet fitter came to measure up and in the general chat they had he said that many charity shops took in second-hand furniture but failing that he could order a skip and shove it all in that. Charlie's human was appalled at the thought of chucking the furniture out but when he had a good look at it, he decided that if the local museum didn't want it, he should get a skip and throw it in that. Trouble was, he didn't know how to get a skip in the first place. He idly picked up his phone, wiped the fine layer of dust off of it and fiddled about with it. When a keyboard appeared he typed the words 'skip hire' and was surprised to see a list of skip hire firms appear. He hurriedly grabbed a piece of paper and wrote the numbers down not realising that he could just click on the highlighted e-mail address straight away through the phone. Out of the half dozen numbers he had copied down he couldn't decide which number to ring when he remembered that his mother used to dowse for things when she couldn't decide one way or another. He was sure she had a crystal on a chain somewhere but hadn't seen it for years. To his surprise he found it almost immediately and thought that somehow, in some way, his mother had led him to it. He shook his head, *my, he was thinking strange things*, he thought, but underneath it all he believed that his mother had shown him and that she was nearby.

He said, "Thanks Mum, I love you," out loud and felt a glow or response to his words and knew, without a shadow of a doubt that she was indeed nearby and looking out for him. He felt happier than he had done in years.

Chapter 8 — Mother Nature

The furniture company phoned to say that they were sorry but the delivery would have to be postponed for a week due to unforeseeable problems. Charlie's human accepted their apology and said that it was OK secretly glad that they had telephoned him as for the past two days he had been worrying about ringing them up to ask if the delivery could be put back because his carpet had yet to be fitted. Feeling rather pleased with himself about how things were turning out and going his way he looked out of the front window and found the skip had been delivered. He was surprised as he was sure he would have heard such a heavy item being dropped in his front garden. He went outside to look at it and saw the name of the firm he had hired it from emblazoned across it.

The skip looked like it had seen better days with its make-up of rust blemishes completely covering it but he supposed it was fit for the job after all, he was only going to chuck furniture in it, he doubted if he would even fill it half way. It didn't need to look posh and shiny to fulfil its task.

Charlie also was feeling quite pleased with himself, he had forgotten up until now how good it felt when his human was happy. He stayed in the forefront of his human's mind as he loaded the furniture onto the skip and helped him use innovative ideas such as placing tin foil underneath the sofa and other pieces of heavy furniture to help him slide them along.

Charlie's human had trouble toppling the sofa into the skip but at last it was done and he thankfully went back indoors mopping his brow as he did so and went and stood in his now empty front room surprised at how big it looked and how vulnerable the room looked without anything in it. He went out of the room and closed the door quietly behind himself fighting down the urge to say sorry to the room for stripping it bare. He shook his head to try to rid himself of these thoughts and went out into the kitchen to have a cup of tea with some lunch and looked at the calendar to see what was coming up or if he had forgotten anything and saw that the carpet fitter was due early the following day, so he had best get up early. He started to worry about oversleeping and missing the carpet man's knock as he was not an early riser and had never got up with the lark in his life. Charlie prompted his human to pick up his phone and helped him to sort out setting the alarm on it. Once done Charlie's human was really chuffed with his familiarization of a modern gadget realising that the only way to get used to it was to use it.

The knock on his door startled him and when he opened it, he found it was a neighbour from two doors down. The neighbour asked him if he minded him taking one of the armchairs out of the skip and Charlie's human agreed and helped him carry it down to his neighbour's house and into their back room. Whilst he waited for the proffered cup of tea, he amused himself by patting the three dogs that were busy waggling their rumps as they sniffed around his ankles. The neighbour tried to shoo the dogs away but was told that everything was OK and that he didn't mind them in the least. Half an hour later he walked back to his home feeling really positive about making a friend with the neighbour and wondering if he should get a dog or two. He didn't want to go so far as to have three dogs like his neighbour but he felt that one dog on its own might get lonely. He had had plenty of times in the past when he had felt lonely and he didn't want a dog of his feeling that way. He mused over the 'a dog of his' phrase and felt really comfortable with the phrase.

Once home, Charlie's human went out into the garden shed feeling in the mood to have a good old sort out. He found loads of tins of paint in dark greens, brown and mauve and carried them out to the skip along with rusty tools, a bicycle frame, an old pram and a lot of broken tiles. He felt he had done a good day's work but was surprised to see that the skip was less than half full until he remembered that one of the armchairs had been taken out of it. Feeling exhausted with his efforts he took himself up to bed for a well-earned rest leaving his mobile phone with its alarm set for the following morning sitting in the kitchen.

The following morning Charlie had a lot of problems trying to get his human to wake up and answer the door and had to first of all settle for him opening a window and shouting down to the person he saw standing on his front path that he would only be a minute, although it was nearer five minutes before he opened the door to let the carpet fitter and his team, who had waited in their van, in. That done, he shot back upstairs cursing the fact that his mobile hadn't woken him up and hurriedly washed and dressed then took a deep breath to compose himself and went downstairs again.

He made himself breakfast and sat and ate it whilst watching the workmen carrying out the old carpet to load it on the skip as agreed. The workmen then mopped the floor and had tea and biscuits whilst waiting for it to dry thoroughly before putting down the underlay.

Charlie enjoyed talking to some of the other shadows recognising one of them from the seminars he attended. All to soon it seemed the job was finished and the team had left, leaving Charlie's human in the transformed front room. He took his shoes and socks off and walked around the room, the thick pile carpet feeling good under his feet. He had the urge to lay down and roll himself over it and did so, giggling uncontrollably and feeling like a kid again. When he finally got up, he was covered in fluff but was feeling great, what would his mum think!

The thought of his mum sobered his high spirits for a time but as he looked around the room, he felt that she would wholeheartedly approve of what he was doing to their family home. Time for a beer he thought but better brush himself off first as he had more wool on him than a sheep!

Whilst down at the pub he bumped into the person who had decorated his front room and she introduced him to her husband. To his surprise, he was not lost for words and thoroughly enjoyed their company and by the rime he left the pub he had arranged for his sitting room and hallway to be decorated. He arranged for them to come around the following day to measure up, then left so that he could have a good old tidy up before they came. He certainly was not going to waste his time washing the walls down, he had learnt from that, after all the wallpaper was going to be stripped off of the walls and thrown away so washing it was a complete waste of time. He wondered why he had bothered to do it at all and thought that perhaps he was ashamed of not looking after his house properly. He hunched his shoulders as these thoughts assailed him then straightened himself up as he strode home, after all, he was now beginning to take charge, things were changing for the better, he felt it in his bones.

The day of the funeral loomed and Charlie's human dressed himself up to the nines and waited for the hearse to arrive. He was getting the hang of his phone now and knew how to set the alarm and play a few games on it that he had managed to download although they were time wasters. He had patted himself on the back remembering to put his phone on the bedside table as he ruefully remembered that the last time he had set the alarm, he couldn't hear it because he had left it downstairs, the silly sod that he was.

The sleek black cars arrived and he strode up the pathway glad that the day was bright after all having a burial on a gloomy rainy day would be the pits. Once in the back of the escort car he looked around his neighbourhood and realised how much it had changed since he was a child. He felt very emotional about it but thought that he was being affected by the fact that today he was going to bury his dad. He realised that he had loved his dad although the fact had been hidden under a lot of irritation and resentment over the years, but when all was said and done, he was still his dad, and now he had no family, he was the dregs.

Upon arriving at the church he was surprised by the amount of people attending, he had no idea that his dad had been so popular or was known by so many people. During the ceremony various elderly people got up to eulogize and he was told of his dad's bravery during the war. He was surprised and humbled as he listened, he knew nothing about it, his mother never spoke of it and neither did his father. All this time he had been living with a hero and he never knew!

The time came for him to say his piece and he got up and went and stood behind the podium when he realised that he had forgotten to look up the words for his poem about daffodils. He stood silently for a time silently cursing his forgetfulness knowing that the congregation would be thinking that he was overcome with remorse as he stood there. He cleared his throat a few times then he looked up and told the audience all the good things that he remembered about his dad, about all the times his dad had play-acted in front of them and made them laugh.

When the service was over, he went and stood by the exit and shook hands or nodded at the congregation as they filed out.

One or two of the ex-servicemen said, "Well done son," and another tipped his hat at him so he thought that he must have done his dad proud and at least passed muster or whatever it was the service people called it.

Later, as he stood by the graveside and had thrown a clump of earth down onto the coffin, he felt sad and glad, sad that a part of him had died but glad that his life had opened up for him and was beckoning. Hopefully his dad would meet up with his mum somewhere and would be happy again.

Although it was a long walk home, he decided against taking the car back and strolled back taking in what was happening around him. His dad came into his mind again and he said hello and asked him if he liked the songs of the little birds he was hearing as he walked down a tree-lined avenue. The many coloured leaves seemed to have a life of their own as they swirled and danced in front of him. He stopped and took it all in for a while, amazed that such a little thing held him transformed.

Charlie was working very hard to make his human aware of Mother Nature, how she continually gave and asked for nothing back. She was there all the time, hidden in plain sight and was so easy to take for granted, to take from and give nothing back in return although the balance of nature was disrupted by such inaction, his human guiltily realised and that he was as much to blame by being in ignorance of her needs as those who deliberately despoiled her.

Charlie's human sat down on an empty bench and suddenly wondered what Mother Nature would look and act like if she was in the form of a woman and suddenly realised, as he looked around him, that she already was there, he just hadn't noticed her, he was already resting in her comforting arms. He realised he had been far too busy living day-to-day and doing mundane things. He closed his eyes and imagined her nurturing him, caring for him along with the billons of other humans who inhabited the earth and he vowed that he would put something back, he didn't know exactly what but doing nothing was not an option.

He became aware that someone was close by and he opened his eyes to see a young woman with a toddler in a pushchair getting ready to sit on the far end of the bench. He smiled at her and shifted along to the other end of the bench so that she had plenty of room and was rewarded with a quick smile in return before she sat down and attended to her toddler's needs. In spite of himself he watched her, worried that she might say something because he was staring but unable to stop himself.

Charlie tried to make his human get up and continue his journey home but was surprised when he met with resistance. After several attempts to get his human moving, he gave up and started chatting to the other human's shadow and was surprised to learn that the shadow knew 37. They had a long and interesting discussion. The shadow of the toddler was, at first, reluctant to join in but then became quite garrulous and took over the conversation.

Charlie's human saw that the young woman had been crying and really wanted to say something but didn't know what to say. She leant forward to tuck the blanket securely around her son and her hair swung forward hiding her face. It was her son who broke the ice although it is doubtful whether he meant to. He lifted his arm and threw his cup out into the pathway. Charlie's human immediately retrieved it and handed it over to the mother who gave a quick smile and mouthed a thankyou at him.

He smiled back then said, "My father was buried here today," by way of explanation of why he was there.

"Roy's dad is here," the young woman whispered, so quietly that it was as if she had not said anything at all.

"Oh," Charlie's human said, thoroughly misunderstanding the young woman and looking around for the child's father.

"His ashes are here," she said looking directly at him. "He never knew he had a son."

"I'm so sorry."

"Don't be, it was a long time ago."

They were both silent for a while, lost in their own thoughts then the young woman remarked on the fine weather and before too long they fell into an easy conversation. They eventually exchanged telephone numbers and parted with a smile. Charlie's human strode homewards thinking how strange life was sometimes. On the day that he had buried his father a new person had come into his life. He should, he thought, be feeling sad at losing his dad but he wasn't, he was glad he had met someone. Once home he got the fire going in the back room and settled himself down in front of the television and fell fast asleep with a half-eaten cheese sandwich resting on his lap. Charlie had worked hard to make his human go upstairs to bed to no effect whatsoever and in the end stopped trying to prevent him sleeping but remained attached in case his human woke up and decided to go upstairs. He didn't want any accidents to befall his human and remained on high alert throughout the night although he desperately wanted to continue his studies. He marvelled that it wasn't so long ago he would have detached and gone to meet the other rogue shadows without caring one iota about whether his human had an accident or not, it just hadn't occurred to him at the time that such a thing could happen, not that he would have cared if it did.

Whilst his human slept, Charlie thought about his conversation with the shadow on the bench with the toddler surprised that the shadow also knew 37. He hadn't thought of 37 recently and wondered how he was doing being the shadow of an albatross. He began to muse over what animal he would like to shadow if he ever got the chance and whilst part of him thought of it a waste of time to do so as he would never be able to make up for not caring and guiding his human through his early years, another part of him decided to do it anyway. He realised that, out of all the precious animals of the earth, that he wanted to be a wolf, a grey wolf preferably, though any colour would do. He spent the rest of the time until his human stirred lost in the joy of his reverie.

Chapter 9 — Blackpool

Charlie's human looked back on his life astonished that in a few short years he had come so far. His house had been completely redecorated inside and out with every room having underfloor heating and his kitchen had totally been revamped. He loved it, every room seemed so light and cared for, quite often he had to pinch himself just to make sure that he wasn't dreaming.

He had booked himself onto a full-time college course regarding computer studies, but had a few hiccups in the beginning. Not being used to nine to five timekeeping or having to do homework. Remembering the problems he had had when he had bought a phone, he labelled himself as not being technology minded and came close to jacking it all in a couple of times. For some reason unknown to himself he stuck to his guns and by the end of the first year was getting reasonable marks and encouraging comments from his tutors.

Although the house was important to him the most important event in his life was that he had found love and it was all down to his father for if he hadn't walked home after his father's funeral, he would never have met Maisie and her little boy, Roy. True, it had taken a lot of hard work to get to where they were but they had moved on from stilted telephone calls to being in each other's company as much as they could.

Charlie had never worked so hard in his life to fulfil his human's potential and spent as much time as he could talking with Maisie's shadow, R45N, so that his human showed the loving caring side of his nature. After all, Maisie was his first love and he didn't want his human to make any mistakes and get the emotional grief and heartache that he had noticed in other humans, although at the time he had noticed he couldn't have cared one way or the other. R45N told him that humans had to make mistakes, it was how they learnt to get along with life and each other but Charlie wasn't so sure, it just sounded daft!

Charlie would have been happy if he only had R45N to live with but RZ2R, Roy's designated shadow, had other ideas, he didn't like Charlie for reasons best known to himself and made sure that his human reciprocated his feelings even though he knew he was wrong to do so for it went against the shadow code.

The relationship went through some sticky patches over the years, mainly due to the fact that Roy screamed his head off every time Charlie's human tried to get to know him better and they even spent some time apart which turned out to be a good thing as they learnt that they needed to be with each other more than they needed to be apart.

The wedding plans were in full swing with Maisie set on Roy being a pageboy although Roy screamed that he didn't want to and said he wanted to go and live with Grandma, Maisie's mother. This was tempting to Maisie as she saw a brief respite from the trauma her son was causing but she knew that she would never go through with it, she definitely would not give in to a five-year-old's demands. Her mother was the only living relative either of them had and they both realised it was important to get her on side, she gave them roots, but, if she refused to attend the wedding then they would both deal with it one way or another.

Maisie's mother had, herself, been a single mother and had believed in the tough love approach to bring her daughter up. When she had found out that Maisie was pregnant, she had done her best to encourage her daughter to 'get rid of it' but was completely taken aback by her daughter's refusal to do so even when threatened with being thrown out on the streets. Even though she hadn't caried out her threat, Maisie's mother couldn't cope with what she saw as a betrayal and wondered where her daughter had got her steel from, after all, she had always meekly agreed to her mother's demands throughout her life.

Charlie tried hard to get on with RZ2R but was continually rebuffed. Roy's shadow thought it was hilarious at the disruption his human was causing and did his best to escalate it. Charlie could see himself, all those years ago when he had left his human to fend for himself whilst he did his own thing and whilst it was true that RZ2R didn't leave his human as much as Charlie had left his, he was manipulating his human, turning him into a puppet to enact his own feelings.

RZ2R blamed Charlie for coming between him and his mother and spoiling his relationship although R45N assured him that there had never been an easy relationship between them in the first place. RZ2R had teamed up with his Grandma's shadow, 88T, and together they had worked very successfully at making Maisie's shadow feel worthless.

Charlie was at a loss to know what to do, he wanted to ask advice but didn't want the powers to be knowing he was having difficulty though he realised that they would know anyway with or without him saying anything as his vibration would have changed. He argued with himself that if the powers that be already knew what was going on then it would be all right to ask for advice but another part of him didn't want to do that. Shadows had obstacles to overcome, it was how they learnt and progressed, a bit like humans learning from mistakes he realised, and he thought that if he continually asked for advice instead of working it out for himself, he would never learn anything. Charlie was surprised at how his thinking was changing but knew that at the moment his thinking wasn't quite right. It was all right to sometimes get help but he couldn't decide if the situation he was in now was one of those times.

The promise of a new bike was a temporary salve but did the trick and Roy was the cutest pageboy ever. The wedding and reception went even better than planned and the newly-weds breathed a sigh of relief as they left for their honeymoon in Blackpool leaving Roy with Maisie's mother for two weeks. Maisie had wanted to take Roy with them, but Charlie's human had put his foot down with a firm hand, it just wasn't going to happen.

When she had been asked to look after Roy for the two weeks the couple would be away on their honeymoon, Maisie's mum had initially dug her heels in and refused point blank but then suddenly had second thoughts as she realised that she would have a chance to turn the screw a little tighter and get Roy to really cause problems between the newly-weds. They both had worked really hard to cause the couple to separate unsuccessfully and needed the honeymoon break to come up with new strategies. It was RZ2R who had been the one to initiate the action by encouraging 88T to agree to put the thoughts in her human's mind to attend the wedding and appear accommodating proffering the carrot that they would have a fortnight in which to hatch out plans of disruption as soon as the wedding was over and the happy couple had set off on their honeymoon.

Charlie knew that something was up and would have preferred not to go away and spent a long time chatting with R45N trying to work out what the other shadows were up to. In the end. R45N got really irritated with him and told him that his continual worry was having a negative effect on his human. That jolted him as he hadn't realised it but soon saw the truth of R45N's words as he recalled his human's restless sleep patterns and a tendency to lose his temper at the slightest provocation. Charlie had noticed the changes taking place in his human but had put them down to his being nervous about the upcoming wedding and was mortified that he had settled for what he thought was the obvious reason for the new behaviour and hadn't dug a little deeper and admitted that he was the cause.

The honeymoon was a dream with the happy couple strolling hand in hand along the promenade completely lost in the wonder of each other but all too soon the honeymoon was over, and they returned home.

Roy was very quiet when he returned from his Grandma's and even the presentation of his new bike didn't brighten his spirits. Maisie worked very hard to find out the cause of the problem but Roy stopped responding to her and most of the time sat staring into the distance. Maisie was beside herself and took him to the doctors' surgery to get checked over, but he was pronounced as fit and well as any other five-year-old child.

Roy's shadow was ecstatic and full of himself. Whilst the happy couple had been on their honeymoon many plans of action had been devised in order to split the newly-weds but he had found the ideal weapon almost by accident. Just before Roy was due to return to his parents he had gone off on a spree with a group of other shadows and left Roy shadowless. The longer he stayed away the less he wanted to return and he began harbouring thoughts of resentment against Roy for keeping him captive and preventing him from living the life a shadow could. RZ2R had tasted what he thought was freedom and he liked it.

Charlie realised what was happening almost immediately and told R45N who tried to get through to Maisie but was continually blocked by stress and anxiety, powerful human emotions that distorted rational thought.

Charlie finally tracked down RZ2R in a group of about thirty other shadows and tried to talk what he thought was reason to him. Charlie wasn't the least bit intimidated and even recognised some of the shadows from when he had hung around in a gang of them.

"Your human is missing you; you need to go back to him and support him."

RZ2R looked around his fellow shadows and laughed. "Good advice coming from a hypocrite."

"What do you mean?" Charlie responded knowing full well what RZ2R meant.

"You left your human for years on end and now you think you have the right to tell me what to do."

"He's suffering without you," Charlie answered in a pleading voice. "He needs you."

"Yeah, well I don't need him," was the response which got sounds of approval from the shadows. "It's about time someone stood up for shadow rights, I'm fed up with being a doormat to a human."

"4Z9 thought the same as you, he was the gang leader and everyone thought that he would never be taken down, that he was unstoppable, but he was stopped, and just look at him now."

Silence ensued for a while. 4Z9 was a legend to many of them and they were trying to hatch plans to free him although all of their efforts had so far come to nothing.

Charlie looked around the group and continued, "I used to worship him, yes, I admit it, to me he could do no wrong but I had a chance to change after he was deposed and I took it. Maybe I could have taken over as leader, who knows, but where would I be now?" Charlie looked around the group most of whom looked elsewhere. "I'd be nowhere, a shadow in a group of shadows."

"4Z9 was a better shadow than you'll ever be."

Charlie looked around himself not knowing the point of origin the comment had come from. "You know, once upon a time I wanted to be like him, he was clever and had such charisma, at one time I would have followed him to the ends of the earth." Charlie's voice broke with emotion but he gathered himself together and said, "If you do go and visit him, I would be very, very, careful as the last time I visited him he tried to change places with me."

Shadows drifted away from the group until Charlie found himself alone with RZ2R who was glaring at him and obviously searching for something cutting to say to him. He was unprepared for what Charlie said next.

"88T made her human put pressure on her daughter to abort your human when she was three months pregnant!"

RZ2R remembered all the good times he had had planning to scupper the newly-weds with the aid of Roy's Grandma but was shocked and couldn't think of anything to say except, "You're a liar, an out and out liar, I don't believe you!"

Charlie left him ranting and raving and returned to his sleeping human. He worked hard to give him happy dreams before leaving to go to a seminar.

Chapter 10 — RZ2R

On the way back from the seminar. "If you don't like yourself how can you make your human like himself?"

Charlie called upon 4Z9 to see how he was getting along and found a very subdued character. He had spent a little time watching him before he approached and had observed 4Z9 huddled in the shade of the statue he had been assigned to.

4Z9 looked up as Charlie approached but didn't say anything. After a few minutes, Charlie hunkered down so that he was on the same level as 4Z9 and simply said, "Hello."

Without warning 4Z9 started to speak and told Charlie about his research of the statue he had been assigned to. Charlie already knew that shadows assigned to immovable objects had, as part of their remit to research what they had been assigned to and that they had to deliver at least 100,000 words or more. 4Z9 shamefacedly remembered laughing as he joked about writing about a telegraph pole and said that no one would ever catch him doing such a thing. At the time he had thought himself at the top of his game and that he was far too clever to be caught.

4Z9's voice was full of wonder as he recounted some of the things he had discovered about the statue. He talked about World War II and how young people had volunteered to join up and fight so that their country would remain free. He had never had that attitude and even just a few short months ago would have sneered at such foolhardiness but something had changed in him as he researched their sacrifices. They had had something to believe in and stood shoulder to shoulder with like-minded fellows proud to defend their land. His statue was of a person who became prime minister towards the end of the war.

4Z9 stopped speaking and looked Charlie straight in the face and said, "I don't know why I was assigned to this statue; I think that they made a mistake as they could have given it to a more deserving shadow but I am glad that they assigned it to me."

Charlie left to return to his human his head full of what had just been said to him. After his initial shock at seeing the change in 4Z9, he felt humbled and grateful for the chance that he had been given for if the teacher had not shocked him with a few well-chosen words all those years ago he might well have found himself in a similar situation.

Charlie's human walked Roy to school on the way to college and gave the little lad a hug and told him that he loved him then stood and watched him as he lined up with the other children and crocodile filed into the building. Once the children had left the playground many of the parents stood in small groups chatting to each other about the joys or miseries of parenting. Charlie noticed, to his surprise that some of them did not have shadows attached and found himself worrying for the little humans. His human gave a smile and a wave to some familiar faces but did not join them and instead continued on towards the college. Once settled down at his desk he found that he had forgotten to give Roy his lunchbox so asked permission to take it to him during the mid-morning break.

From a window in the school corridor he watched Roy sitting by himself in the corner of the class and refusing to join in. He had the urge to burst into the classroom and take his son, his Roy, home. He made a move forward as if to carry out his thought then stopped as if he had had second thoughts. In reality it was Charlie who had stopped him. Charlie had seen RZ2R staring into the classroom further down the passageway. He made a movement towards RZ2R but stopped when he saw the shadow edge away from him.

He simply said, "He needs you, look at him. We all need you to help him. Please help him."

RZ2R looked at him for a moment then turned as if to move away when Charlie repeated, "We need you, we can't do this without you. Don't you realise you are the only one that can help?"

There was such emotion in his voice that RZ2R stopped and looked at him then, without another word floated into the classroom and reattached himself to Roy. Charlie immediately saw the change in Roy who left his lonely position and came and sat in the storytelling circle with the rest of his classmates to hear about the amazing adventures of a white rabbit called Legolas.

Charlie's human though had no idea of the undercurrent activity. All he saw was his son getting up and joining the storytelling group. He put a hand up to his mouth and gave a sigh of relief, thankful that he hadn't burst into the classroom and make a fool of himself and perhaps make things worse. He took the lunchbox to the reception office and left it there then returned to college.

Later that day as Charlie was having his lunch, he wondered at how things worked out, for if he hadn't forgotten to give Roy his lunchbox, he would never have had to return to the school so would not have known that RZ2R was there. He briefly wondered why RZ2R was at the school but decided to not go into things too deeply and just accept the outcome.

On collecting Roy from school Roy was full of the things he had done at school and presented his dad with a painting he had done.

"Oh, that's lovely, what is it?"

"It's a rabbit, look there it is."

"Oh yes, thank you, it's lovely. We'll show it to Mummy when we get home."

"Can I have a rabbit, a white one, Daddy?" Roy looked up into his dad's face waiting for an answer.

"Let's ask Mummy when we get home," said Charlie's human thinking that by the time they reached home Roy would have forgotten all about it.

Roy seemed happy with the answer and said, "I'm going to call it Legless."

"Legless!"

"Yes," said Roy and skipped ahead swinging his empty lunchbox to and fro. When he reached the corner, he stopped and waited for his dad as he had been told countless times to do still swinging his lunchbox.

A black van, cutting the corner as it turned left into the road, caught his outstretched arm and spun him around. The occupants of the van must have known they had hit something or someone by the noise of the connection but did no more than to accelerate away. Roy's dad watched his little man crumple to the ground in horror and ran the few steps needed to reach him and knelt beside Roy screaming his name.

Later at the hospital, Roy had the length of his right arm encased in plaster. The hospital had given him a full examination and had decided to keep him in overnight just to be certain. Roy didn't want his dad to leave him but was told to close his eyes and go to sleep and when he woke up his Daddy and Mummy would be there. Charlie's human waited until he was sure that Roy was fast asleep then returned home and told Maisie, who had just returned home from her yoga class, what had happened and she insisted on returning to the hospital straight away all the while continually asking for reassurance that Roy had nothing more than a broken arm.

The hospital allowed Roy to go home the following day and he asked to go to school so that he could show off his plaster and was disappointed when his parents said no.

Over the coming days the change in Roy was remarkable and Charlie repeatedly told RZ2R what an amazing shadow he was. Charlie watched the little boy flourish but every now and then gave himself verbal grief as he remembered how he had been when his human was young. He couldn't believe the joy this young person gave him and knew that he had been given a second chance.

R45N told him that it was useless looking backwards as it would make the journey forwards difficult if not impossible as he would be dragging a lot of unnecessary baggage in the form of guilt with him. It wasn't his fault that Roy had had his arm broken and he should stop raking over old ground, the past had passed. He now had the opportunity to watch Roy grow and he should take it with open arms, accept that he was fallible but was willing to learn. Charlie was astounded at her wisdom and counted himself lucky that they had found each other.

A week later, Charlie's human took Roy back to school to show off his plaster cast and his schoolfriends had a fine old time writing and drawing on it. When it was finally time for him to leave, he wanted to stay but wasn't allowed to. Roy sulked all the way home and had a big strop the minute he got indoors, so much so that, for a minute or two, Charlie feared that Roy was returning to his old ways.

Christmas was looming and Charlie's human had taken Roy out to buy presents and returned home heavily laden with shopping bags to find Maisie being sick in the bathroom. She laughed at their concern but over the next few days she continued being sick and in the end Charlie's human pressured her to see the doctor.

"There is nothing wrong with me, I'm just pregnant that's all," she told the concerned faces of her husband and son.

Roy wasn't sure if what his mother had said was a good thing or not so looked to his father for a clue of how to react.

He saw his father's amazed face then watched him leap around the room, shouting, "I'm going to be a daddy."

Roy copied him, much to the amusement of his mother. When they had calmed down and insisted she lay down and rest she told Roy that he wasn't going to be a daddy but he would soon have a little brother or sister. Roy decided then and there that he wanted a baby brother and the family of three, soon to be four, hugged each other and enjoyed the moment.

Charlie sat with RZ2R staring out into the night and amazed that he got on so well with him now, it seemed such a short time ago when they were busy firing daggers at each other. Maisie's shadow, R45N, joined them and they shared their thoughts about Maisie's pregnancy and talked about the new shadow, ZUP2, that had appeared on the scene but as yet had kept a distance from them. Charlie stated that at the rate they were going they would soon have to get a bigger house. With all their humans settled they then left for their various seminars.

Charlie only listened with half an ear to his seminar, there was something nagging at him that he couldn't quite get hold of. There were a few times when he almost had it but it slipped away into the ethos.

"Penny for them, Charlie."

Charlie looked up then around him surprised that apart from the teacher and himself there was nobody around. One moment there had been hundreds of shadows and now they had gone. "I've got a thought that I can't quite get hold of and I try to leave it be and pretend that it's OK for it to come into my head when it's good and ready but as soon as I realise I've nearly got it, it fades away."

The teacher smiled. "Ah yes, thoughts have an energy all of their own and sometimes it seems that they simply don't want to be thought about."

Charlie thought that the teacher's response was too deep for him to grasp at the moment and simply said, "I'm sure it's really important though."

The teacher merely smiled at him and faded away and Charlie left also briefly calling in on 4Z9 on the way before continuing home to attach to his human.

As the days went passed, Maisie began to feel a whole lot better and she and Roy decorated the house whilst her husband was at college. Roy tried to inflate a blow-up Father Christmas which went down the minute he stopped puffing, which had

Maisie in fits of laughter much to Roy's chagrin. In the end, his mother found him a bicycle pump and helped him just a tiny bit so that before long the jolly figure was ready to take pride of place in the front garden. Roy got over excited at all the twinkling lights and Maisie had to insist he take a rest and though Roy protested that he wasn't in the least bit tired, he was soon fast asleep.

Charlie's human had meant to buy a Christmas tree on the way home from college but forgot all about it until he arrived home and saw the expectancy then disappointment on Roy's face. After promising to go with Roy the following day to buy one he sat down to his dinner congratulating his wife on over doing the decorations in a good, humoured way. Maisie threw a box of crackers at him in response, and they ended up pulling on one of the crackers with its contents diving into his dinner.

True to his word, Charlie's human and Roy went out to buy a tree and in the end, they struggled home with one which only just fitted into their front room. Roy decorated all the lower branches with his one good arm and soon the family stepped back to examine their efforts. The lights flickered on and off a few times then stayed off and Roy wailed in disappointment whilst his dad went through every bulb to see it was screwed in properly. Of course it was the very last one that was at fault but before long Roy was shouting excitedly and asking when Father Christmas was coming excitedly telling his parents that Father Christmas was going to bring him a rabbit.

With all the things that were happening Charlie's human had completely forgotten about Roy asking about if he could have a rabbit and to be fair a lot had happened since that had caused the fact to slip his mind. Maisie looked meaningfully at him glancing towards Roy and back to him a few times then left the room, Roy picked up on the vibes between his parents and said in a low voice "Father Christmas is not going to bring me a rabbit, is he?"

Charlie's human pulled his son towards him wondering what to say with thoughts of Father Christmas not having enough room for rabbits streaming through his head.

He cleared his throat a few times then said in a gruff voice what Father Christmas would have been proud of. "Animals are not presents, they never have been nor should they ever be. They become part of a family in order to teach humans."

"Are we humans?"

"Yes."

"Teach humans! What like my teacher does?" said Roy.

"In a way it is though in a way it isn't."

Roy stepped back and looked at his father and said, "Grown-ups are weird," before running off to find his mother to tell her he was starving.

Charlie's human sat back on the sofa totally drained, *kids*, he thought, *who'd have them*!

All too soon Christmas came and went, one moment the expectation was peaking as the day was eagerly awaited and then, in a flurry it was gone, leaving few really happy with what they had given or received or aware of the true meaning of the day. The charity shops were filled almost to bursting point as they took in unwanted presents, purchases that, at one time, had seemed inspired but, in reality had been bought in a last-ditch attempt to by something, anything.

Roy was ecstatic with his shiny new bike but kept demanding that the stabilizers be removed as he had seen friends in his class riding without them and wanted to do the same. His plaster cast had finally been removed and he had had to relearn to use two arms again so was only taken out for short rides around the block whilst he built up the strength in his arm. He wasn't interested in any other toys and kept pestering his parents to take him out all the while insisting that he was strong enough. His parents held hands and watched him wobble along, their hearts brimming with love.

Charlie's human returned for the final few terms of college and Maisie had the difficult job of keeping her son actively engaged until it was time for him to return to school. Her pregnancy was going well although she was told that she needed to take time out for herself sometimes.

When the family had finally settled down for the night, the three shadows detached themselves from their humans and talked over the day before going on to their different seminars. ZUP2 had come closer to them as Maisie's pregnancy was progressing but still didn't seem to want to mix with them. Charlie's human had been getting grumpy and short-tempered lately though Charlie knew that it was not down to the human, it was down to him. The evasive worrying thought that he had been chasing around his mind for months had suddenly revealed itself and Charlie didn't know what to do with it. He knew he should share it with R45N and RZ2R but until he had got it sorted out in his mind, he didn't know how to broach it, it wasn't something that you could suddenly drop in casual conversation.

These were his jumbled thoughts. Humans didn't know that they had shadows to guide them although shadows knew that they had humans to guide. A human whose shadow did not guide them, who left them to pretty much get on with life by themselves could live on the outskirts of society finding it hard if not impossible to fit in. A shadow who left his human to get by as best he could whilst he did his own thing would pay the price once his human had died unless he had tried to change and help his human. The price the shadow would pay was that he would become a shadow to an inanimate object for maybe thousands of years until it was proved by intense research that a change had occurred in him.

If a shadow had worked hard to help his human but his human had resisted all efforts to be helped it was possible that the shadow could be reassigned to another human or assigned to Mother Nature so that they could have the privilege of becoming the shadow of a tree or one of her billions of plant species. Charlie had never ever considered that he could one day become the shadow of a tree and he was awestruck by the possibility and had spent his spare time reading about them to find out more. He had labelled trees as 'still life' but he found that he couldn't have been more wrong, trees were alive and gave sustenance to hundreds of other creatures whether they provided shade or a home or food but what really got Charlie excited was the fact that trees communicated with each other.

All these things Charlie had learnt during his life but he hadn't learnt about the question that was troubling him. He knew how humans recreated themselves, he had seen it many times but what he didn't know was where had shadows come from in the first place, what was the initial event that had caused a shadow to be formed. Surely shadow history must be stored somewhere for the students to learn about but in all the seminars he had attended the subject had never been broached. He had never thought of it before but now he couldn't stop thinking about it, it seemed such an obvious question. He had been content with the variety of seminars on offer but now he had thought about where shadows had originated from he couldn't let it go but who could he talk to, who could he share his thoughts with? If he spoke to one of the tutors would something bad happen to him because he had dared to ask. Would he be banished to a place were no shadow had ever been before or worse? Charlie tormented himself with the endless possibilities and his human became more and more, bad tempered. He knew that humans could kill humans and he wondered if shadows could kill shadows. The thought of never seeing the other shadows that had become such a large part of his life was tearing him apart but more than anything the thought of being parted from his human was unbearable and made him realise how much he had come to love him.

Chapter 11 — Time Bubble

Maisie was in hospital having contractions and her shadow, R45N, was having a rough time as she tried everything she knew to help her human. Maisie was, apparently, stuck in the second stage of labour, so although the contraction was regular her dilation didn't increase so no progress was being made. ZUP2 floated nearby, helpless and wondering if her human would ever be born. Charlie's human didn't know what to do but managed to continually get in the way as his wife was checked out. He felt guilty at putting her through so much pain and vowed that he never would again.

Maisie had begun to call her husband 'Bear' because of his continual bad temper and the nickname stuck so that even Roy called his dad Bear. She thought that the reason why he was so short-tempered was that he was worried for her and their baby and she loved him even more for it, after all, it showed he cared.

Roy was staying with the family of one of his schoolfriends who just happened to have a ginger Rex rabbit called Gideon and Roy spent every moment that he could stroking or feeding the rabbit and even volunteering to clean out the large hutch in which the rabbit lived with his sister, named Spirit. Roy knew that his mother was in hospital so that the baby could come out of her tummy and be his baby brother or sister but was distracted by the thoughts he had of owning a rabbit so much so that he barely listened to his dad when he called him from hospital to see if he was all right.

Charlie had to shelve the thoughts he was having as his human was full on at the moment, not able to sleep for more than a couple of hours at a time. Bear looked to be in a much worse condition than his wife with his red-rimmed eyes, blotchy face and being desperately in need of a shave. He couldn't eat, he couldn't sleep but he could weep and he did this every time he spoke to his wife gripping her hands so hard it hurt.

Whilst he was being miserable at her bedside she was checked again and suddenly all guns were blazing and she was whisked away into the labour ward. Bear tried to go into the ward with her but was firmly told that if he did so he had to pull himself together and remember the breathing exercises that they had had instruction on when they attended the prenatal classes. This brought Bear up short as he had forgotten all about the exercises and techniques they learnt and from that moment he was able to assist his wife and encourage her when she was told to push. He kissed her hand and wiped her brow and told her how beautiful she was and all of a sudden, the baby's head was presented and his wife was being told to pant not push, then was told to make one last big effort.

Moments later, Maisie was holding the baby and Bear was holding them both. He walked beside the bed as it was pushed to the maternity ward and once his wife was settled, he made his way home and called in to collect Roy and told him that the baby had been born.

"Is he a brother, have I got a brother?" Roy asked and Bear said he didn't know; all he knew was that his wife had given birth. Roy was not in the least impressed and asked if he could stay with his friend a bit longer and his parents agreed saying that they thought it was a good idea as it would give Bear the chance to catch up on some much-needed sleep.

When Bear had showered and collapsed into bed, Charlie detached himself and went to the hospital to talk to the new shadow, ZUP2 who welcomed the approach now that his human had survived the birth. He spent a long time chatting with the shadow and reliving the moment of birth before he went to his classes. He found that there was a seminar called 'living in accommodation with other shadows' and thoroughly enjoyed it and asked a lot of questions. He was worried that their house, although it was a big house, might be getting overcrowded now that it had eight residents in it but his teacher dispelled the idea saying that after all there were really only four humans living in the house and that shadows, with their ability to shrink or expand would be able to fit in anywhere after all walls were no boundary to them, they could go anywhere unless, of course, they were restricted by the shadow council and permanently attached to a still object!

Charlie spent a long time mulling over this information and was only made aware of the passing time when he felt the vibration of Bear stirring and quickly hurried back and attached himself before Bear fully awoke.

As Bear went into the kitchen to make his breakfast his phone made little beeping noises as if to welcome him. He picked it up and scrolled through it and read the message that he had left for himself, today was the anniversary of his mother's death. He stared hard at the phone and was still staring at it when the screen had faded. Melancholy and guilt began to creep over him as he whispered he was sorry, he had forgotten. He didn't want to tell her that he had forgotten the anniversary because he had been busy at the hospital as he didn't want to give an excuse although, in reality, it was not an excuse, it was a justified reason. Bear had one dreadful thought and was shocked at himself for thinking that he was glad that their new baby hadn't been born on the anniversary of his mother's death. After a while, Bear went on to tell his mother about the new baby and all about Roy and his wanting a rabbit called Legless and he found himself laughing for the first time ever as he talked to her. He realised that he had no reason to be sad, his mum was in heaven, the place where he would one day meet up with her if he tried very hard to do what he felt was best for his family.

Bear woke up with a cramp in his arm and realised he had fallen asleep on the kitchen table. He stretched his arm out then glanced at the clock and suddenly became activated, it was mid-afternoon already. He collected Roy from his friend's house offering profuse apologies for being so late and walked with Roy to the flower shop to choose flowers for his mum. Bear chose a huge bunch of flowers and Roy chose a cactus for the baby and Bear managed, with a tremendous effort from Charlie to say nothing.

Maisie was looking better but had had a sleepless night as she wasn't managing to breast feed very well and thought that she was failing as a mother. Bear laughed at this then realised he had put his foot in it as he should have said something along the lines that these things take time and that she was a wonderful mother, after all, look how Roy had turned out. To cover his confusion he thrust the bunch of flowers at her and was relieved to see that she loved them.

Whilst Bear was giving his mother the flowers Roy went over to the sleeping baby and stared down at it then told it he had bought a cactus for it and waited for a response. He told it a second time as he thought it had not heard him the first time then prodded it awake. The baby gave a loud yell and Roy backed quickly away glancing at his parents as he did so.

He said, "I bought the baby a cactus," by way of explanation for the baby crying and was relieved to see his parents smiling at him.

Bear took the cactus from Roy and his mother spread her arms wide to encourage him to come to her then gave a long hug to her favourite boy, the best boy in the world then tickled him to make him wriggle and giggle.

As soon as Charlie turned up that night for a seminar, he was told he had to go to Time Bubble Eleven and wait for his assessor. This was the first time Charlie had ever been asked to go into a Truth/Time Bubble and he grew increasingly anxious as he waited by Number Eleven although he had overheard stories about them from other shadows who had claimed to have been in them. Apparently, you could be in there months or years but the time would be the same when you stepped out as when you stepped in. This was very close to the truth although none of the shadows actually believed it was possible. Rumours had been rife in the gang of rogue shadows that Charlie used to float around with though not one of them had ever been near one. Most of them, like him, had ignored the call for a random assessment thinking they were far too clever to be caught out that way.

With his mind working overtime Charlie was on the verge of leaving when his assessor appeared, opened the Time Bubble and gestured for Charlie to enter it first. Charlie would have much preferred to follow his assessor in for then he would have the option of scarpering if the need took him.

The questions started as soon as the Bubble was sealed. "What was the purpose of shadows? Can shadows influence human action? Explain how humans can ignore shadow instruction?"

The questions were fired at him like the bullets from a machine gun with no time allowed for thinking before speaking.

In the midst of all the questions one was thrown in which, for a brief time, made him speechless as he tried to work out what was behind the question. "Explain your former relationship with 4Z9."

Relationship, he thought, *why is the assessor asking me that, I was a gang member that's all.* Further questions were fired at him before he could answer. "Explain how a shadow could be downgraded to still life? Why do shadows need to respect their human? Why do you still visit 4Z9? How did shadows evolve?"

Charlie answered the last question, very similar to the one he had been worrying over for days, without thinking. "Shadows evolved when the light from above shone."

All of a sudden it seemed Charlie was standing outside the Bubble.

The assessor said, "See you again soon Charlie," then floated away leaving Charlie confused and wondering what was wrong, one moment his assessor had been approaching him and next moment he was floating away from him. Why was that! Had his assessor changed his mind or something. He had no idea of ever being inside the Bubble whatsoever, just as the designers of the Bubble had intended. Charlie needed to go away and think as for some reason he felt like he had been wrung out then hung up to dry but moments later, he found himself in the 'If you don't like yourself how can you make your human like himself?' seminar along with R45N and ZUP2.

The three shadows returned home together and RZ2R came out to meet them and told them that he thought that Roy was coming down with something and asking them about the seminar they had attended. When Charlie told them he had been to a Truth/Time Bubble they started bombarding him with questions but Charlie, for the life of him, couldn't remember anything that had happened apart from being approached by an assessor one minute then immediately being dismissed by him. His friends thought he was being secretive and had been sworn to silence but Charlie insisted it wasn't the case, if he knew anything he would tell them. He didn't know what was going on and though he tried hard to think events over he couldn't remember going into the Bubble or having a series of questions fired at him which was a shame really as he could have had certain peace of mind in knowing that deep inside himself he knew the answer to the question that had been causing him concern over the last week or so.

ZUP2 left for the hospital with R45N leaving Charlie and RZ2R to worry about Roy who was twisting and turning in bed and sweating profusely. Charlie reattached himself to Bear and helped him get up and attend to his son's needs, wiping him down and giving him cool drinks. There were no spots visible on him so Bear could discount some of the common childhood ailments. He rang Maisie to say that he couldn't visit that day and explained Roy's systems to her and she gave him guidelines of how to look after Roy, told him that the baby was fine but that she also had a raised temperature that the hospital was keeping an eye on so perhaps it was just as well they couldn't visit her.

As he put his mobile down, Bear heard Roy calling and rushed up the stairs two at a time and found his son lying in bed covered in vomit where he had thrown up. Bear was in a panic with what to do first and wished with all his heart that Maisie was there to take charge. Should he clean Roy first then do the bedding or do the bedding then attend to Roy? Bear had no idea how he got things sorted out but somehow, he did. He looked down at his son snuggled up in a warm clean bed, stroked his hair and told him how much he loved him then got on with doing the laundry.

Whilst sorting out the laundry Bear had a panic attack and sank down onto the floor in the laundry room dizzy and sweating, his mind whirling. He forced himself to breath slowly and deeply all the while telling himself that everything was going to be all right but it took a long time for him to calm, and even then, he still shivered occasionally. He thought that perhaps he should go and see a doctor to see if anything could be done about having panic attacks but was worried in case the doctor told him he was wasting his time. Bear told himself to pull himself together, first of all he needed to be there for his family, he didn't have time to be ill. His son and his new baby were both ill and both had raised temperatures, what was going on! He consoled himself that at least his wife was in the safest place and phoned through to the surgery to get advice on the symptoms his son was displaying or get a home visit.

Roy spent most of that day sleeping, albeit not peacefully, and Bear had his work cut out attending to him and worrying over him. Roy never murmured when he was given a strip wash and his sodden bedding was changed yet again.

As Bear pulled the duvet over him Roy opened his eyes and said, "Hello Dad," before closing them again but this time his sleep was restful and his flushed cheeks gradually returned to normal.

None of the shadows went to seminars that night as they worked hard to make the experience of life worthwhile for their humans, helping them to realise that there was strength in family unity.

Chapter 12 — Abduction

4Z9 had managed to swop places with one of his former rogue gang members and was enjoying his freedom. It was easy to trick a former friend but he knew he didn't have long as the vibration change would alert the S.A.S. (shadow authenticity squad). It was supposed to be impossible to escape, however briefly, from a still form but 4Z9, with plenty of time on his hands had worked out how to accomplish it. He felt sorry for the shadow he had tricked as he had not the slightest intention of returning.

Meanwhile, in the hospital, Maisie had also developed a high temperature but didn't improve the way her son Roy had and continued to be violently sick and for a time was isolated in case the condition she had was contagious. Bear didn't want to take the baby home as he didn't feel he could cope very well and was having enough trouble looking after Roy, so the baby was moved to the hospital nursery after being thoroughly examined and found to be free of the condition that was ravaging her mother.

Once Roy was strong enough to go out, Bear took him shopping for a rabbit telling him that his new sister Daisy wanted to give him a present. Roy was not a fool but pretended to be taken in as he wanted a rabbit more than anything else and if he had to pretend to believe the lie that was spilling out of his dad's mouth then so be it.

By the time they had visited the fourth shop, Bear's patience was beginning to wear thin. Roy had set his heart on a ginger rabbit but they were scarce and search as they might they didn't come across one. In the end Roy settled for a fluffy all-black buck rabbit and decided to call him Apache there and then.

Bear had already set up the hutch and run in the back garden ensuring that it was as fox-proof as possible and had ordered enough food for a rabbit army as he wasn't sure how much rabbits ate and didn't want him to go without. He found that he had to store the food in metal bins as the rats made short work of the paper food sacks that he had stored in the shed.

Apache was placed in his home and Roy and Bear stood back and watched him inspect it, their faces beaming as Apache took his first bite from one of the carrots.

Charlie watched the rabbit's shadow with wonder, he couldn't believe that they finally had an animal shadow in the household. He spent a lot of time distracted by the new shadow and didn't fully concentrate on Bear until Bear got a call from the hospital the following morning asking him to go in as a matter of urgency. He asked why but the hospital simply told him to go there straight away.

Bear couldn't think straight, what on earth was wrong! There had to be something wrong as they wouldn't have called him. He asked his neighbour from two doors down to come around to look after Roy for a short while explaining that he had had an urgent call from the hospital and left as soon as his neighbour arrived telling him to help himself to anything he needed.

Bear sat beside Maisie in her hospital bed and held her hand and told her that he loved her, he needed her, as tears rolled down his face. The doctors had told him prior to going into her room that Maisie was improving, she had finally stabilized, and Bear closed his eyes and sent up a silent prayer of thanks.

His relief didn't last long as when he left Maisie, he was called aside by a doctor who had two policemen with him and was told that his daughter, Daisy, was missing from the Nursery. Bear couldn't contain himself and exploded with accusations as the doctor tried to explain to him what had happened and what they were doing about it. Eventually Bear started to listen and agreed with the doctor that it would be prudent not to tell Maisie just yet then went into a side room with the two police officers who brought him up to date with everything they had done so far after asking him where he had been during the previous twelve hours. The footage on the hospital cameras, all of which were in good working order, was at that very moment being scrutinized and they assured Bear that they would get back in touch with him as soon as they had more information.

Bear was relieved that Maisie didn't know that their daughter was missing, then horrified to have such thoughts. He berated himself although he knew it wouldn't do any good, he should have taken Daisy home when he had had the chance and now, because he had thought he couldn't cope with her needs, she could be anywhere, she could have been left dumped in a wheelie bin or was at that very moment being hurt by someone who hated babies, his mind tortured him with worst possible scenarios, each one worse than the thought before.

Charlie worked very hard to keep Bear on track and eventually Bear managed to make it home after declining a lift there from the police. What on earth was he going to tell Roy!

Roy listened to his father telling him that his sister had been taken away by someone and nodded his head as if he understood. Daisy had been taken away by a stranger, he had heard all about them, at school. He put his arms around the shuddering shoulders of his dad then updated him on what his rabbit had been up to.

Bear shouted at his son, the first time he had ever raised his voice to him, as he said he didn't want to hear about some stupid rabbit, his daughter, Roy's sister, was missing and didn't he understand that. Roy stepped back in shock then turn and fled to his room and threw himself on his bed shouting that he hated his dad forever.

Bear visited Maisie again that afternoon after settling Roy with some colouring books in the guest room. Roy had kicked up a fuss and said he didn't want to go to the hospital, he wanted to stay with his rabbit and it took a huge effort on Bear's part not to shout at his son again. He finally got his son to accompany him when he said that he was worried that Apache might be lonely and that perhaps they should get him a companion.

No sooner than the words had left his mouth that he wished he hadn't said them after all he had enough on his plate at the moment but Roy flew into his dad's arms and hugged him fiercely and said, "Thanks, Dad," so Bear knew that he had committed himself.

He really meant what he had said to Roy but his promise faded into the back of his mind as his priority was the welfare of his daughter.

Bear had decided against telling Maisie that her daughter was missing but, in the end, broke down when she kept asking him what was wrong, what was he hiding from her. He told her and then had to call in a nurse to help calm her as she had initially seemed to take the news quite calmly then suddenly started screaming and trying to rake him with her nails whilst using previously unheard-of language.

Charlie had been doing a lot of thinking during this time and that night he called the shadows together for a meeting when their humans were settled. The shadows met up and were introduced to R1, the shadow from Apache the rabbit and even though it was a solemn occasion they couldn't help but be impressed by R1.

They discussed what had happened and what they could do about it. Various ideas were put forward then Charlie took the floor and said that they should use their advantage as shadows, they should look for and contact ZUP2 although he was concerned that ZUP2 hadn't made any attempt to contact them. Decision made, they spread out and contacted other shadows who contacted other shadows. Charlie went to a seminar and put a notice on the board and stood up in class and asked for help and was overwhelmed by the shadows' response.

Charlie had had it in the back of his mind that the shadow or shadows of whoever had taken Daisy would be alerted to the concerted effort to find her. He didn't know how many shadows were in on the abduction or if it was just one but he decided the risk of them knowing that a shadow army was looking for Daisy was worth it even if they did try to warn their humans.

ZUP2 was in a quandary knowing that the human baby was in danger but not knowing what to do about it. The shadow of the young teenager who had taken the child was very rarely present so there was no chance of persuading the shadow to make his human return the child. ZUP2 was unaware of the concerted effort of many shadows were trying to find the location he was in and felt very much alone. Wild thoughts assailed his mind of plans to save his human all by himself although he knew that was an impossibility. He decided that the best thing that he could do was to remain attached to the baby although initially he nearly detached himself so that he could go and get help from shadows of humans living nearby. He decided that the baby was too young to leave on her own.

The young girl who had taken the baby seemed now to be unaware of what she had done and was confused by the baby's presence. It had been so easy to take the baby from the hospital in the early hours of that morning and at the time it had seemed like a good idea for her to have someone to love and something who loved her in return. The cold reality of what she had done hit her quickly. Whilst the baby was asleep, she had held it and told it she loved it but when the baby woke up and started crying it was as if it was finding fault with her. She had the urge to throw it across the room to stop it crying but in the end put it in a back room and covered it with blankets. The thought came to her that perhaps she should take it back to where she had found it but decided it was too risky and any way she couldn't, she had her needs to look out for first, she needed to earn her next fix.

FLR2, the young girl's designated shadow, had briefly returned to the squat when he felt his human was distressed and though these days, he rarely responded to the signal of his human the urge to return was strong. He watched her trying to mother a baby, stroking it and singing stupid songs to it. FLR2 had thought that his despicable human child was nursing a doll until cries emerged from the little form she was cuddling. He watched her for a little while, contempt turning down the edges of his mouth then left the squat not questioning where the child had come from.

FLR2 joined in with some other shadows trying to intimidate the shadows attached to humans who were passing by them. He had no love for his human, or any humans, come to that. He despised her, not realising that his not taking responsibility for his human was one of the main factors that caused her to be like she was. The shadow group he floated around with enjoyed nothing more than a road accident where humans were killed or badly injured and derided shadows who remained attached to their humans for most of their lives or others who went to seminars to learn how best to help their humans. 'What about the needs of shadows' was the cry that went around the group as well as 'humans should be helping us not the other way around'.

Some of the shadows who occasionally attended seminars joined the group in the early morning and said that a call had gone out for shadows to track down ZUP2 whose human had been taken whilst in a hospital nursery.

FLR2 said nothing but listened very carefully to what was being said before moving away from the group to give himself thinking time. Apparently, it was Charlie who was putting out the call to find the baby and there was only one shadow called Charlie, all the shadows knew him or knew of him, he had been a cohort of 4Z9 and was a legend that every rogue shadow aspired to. Charlie had dropped out of sight recently as had 4Z9 and there was a lot of activity among the shadows to take their places.

FLR2 felt nervous and excited, perhaps this was the time when he could finally show the group what he was made of and earn their respect. That's all he wanted really, to be revered, not much to ask but he had been given a stupid girl human and there had seemed no way for him to get noticed by his fellow shadows until now, now she had actually done something that could make the name FLR2 be spoken of in awe, perhaps he should reattach to her. The thought made him shiver for what shadow in their right mind would ever want to be attached to a human!

FLR2 floated back to the squat and hovered near his human, taking in her dishevelled appearance and the empty misshaped drink cans strewn about her comatose form. A feeling a superiority crept over him and he realised that perhaps he should feel sorry for her for being a human and not being a shadow. He floated through to the back room and saw the human baby on the floor appearing to be fast asleep. He went closer to check that the human was still breathing and was accosted by ZUP2 who demanded he get his human to take the human baby back to the hospital.

FLR2 was caught by surprise initially having given no thought to the possibility that the baby would have a shadow but quickly recovered his composure and backed off saying, "No chance," before quickly moving away.

He didn't have much time he knew as the S.A.S. would have picked up the change in the human baby's vibration and would be honing in on her even now and, on top of all that, there was Charlie to think about. He suddenly realised what all the other shadows knew, he was spineless. Yes, he was all right when he could manipulate the weak and helpless or carry out instructions from superior shadows, but he had no vision, no planning ability. He could dream all he liked about being a revered leader but he knew that that was never going to happen. Here he was with a bomb in his lap that was about to go off and he was going to get caught in the blast!

Charlie was surprised when he was accosted by FLR2 and recognised him immediately as one of the dregs that hung around on the edges of shadow groups. He saw how nervous FLR2 was and reckoned that his previous reputation was still rife amongst shadow groups. He waited patiently for FLR2 to speak wondering how he even had the nerve to approach him and watched as the other shadow tried to compose himself enough to speak.

"I can take you to the missing baby."

Charlie closed the distance between him and FLR2 instantly causing him to shrink away.

He loomed over the cringing shadow as he hissed, "*What*. What did you say?"

FLR2 was frightened as he realised that approaching Charlie hadn't been one of his best ideas. He shrank down even further and tried to speak but his voice refused to come out of his mouth. Charlie looked at the quivering form and realised that he had better change his approach if he was going to get any information out of the shadow. He asked the other shadow in a much quieter voice what his name was.

"FLR2."

"FLR2?"

"Yes."

"Well FLR2 what do you know about the missing human baby?"

FLR2 knew that Charlie's softer tone was not a sign of weakness but a way of getting information out of him but knowing that couldn't stop him spilling the beans once he had started and he revealed every last detail before taking Charlie with him back to the squat. Charlie dismissed FLR2 who almost bowed before fleeing away then floated passed the human girl still comatose on the floor and met ZUP2 in the back room where they had a brief but joyous reunion with ZUP2 informing him that the baby, Daisy, was hungry but was all right before turning their thoughts to how to notify the humans where the baby was.

The S.A.S. arrived and Charlie and ZUP2 brought them up to date and Charlie was abruptly dismissed after telling them what he knew.

It was an hour later when a dishevelled human girl carrying a bundle close to her chest approached the reception desk in the local hospital. The hospital foyer was practically deserted during the early hours of the morning and the girl stood out all the more because of it.

The words, "I've got the stolen baby," initially startled then galvanised the receptionist who pressed the alarm button for hospital security to come running. If aware of the commotion she was causing the girl made no sign and stood still staring at the receptionist who was now phoning the nursery. The girl allowed a nurse to take the baby from her and meekly followed the security guard into a side room where she sat and spoke to the guard.

For the first time in her young life she felt what it was like to be human, felt that she was a part of the human race and was not just a bystander. The S.A.S. operative who had attached to her to animate her worked hard on her belief system, telling her well done for returning the baby and that she mattered as much as any human mattered. The operative wouldn't stay with her but she would be assigned a new shadow, one who had gone through 'still' life and had reformed to know that the purpose of shadows was to ensure that their humans reached their potential.

As she was a minor, she didn't feel the full weight of the law and instead found herself cared for by the system that had previously known nothing about her. Regular meals, a safe place to sleep and people who she could talk to which began the gentle process of transforming her.

FLR2 tried to get back to his human blustering that he loved her and wanted to help her but all to no avail. He found himself sentenced to be attached to a still life, attached to a telegraph pole on a rarely used highway miles from anywhere.

Once there, FLR2 started to go through all the stages of attachment to a still life form that is, blaming everyone else for his predicament, anger and threats, loneliness and despair until the realisation came, if ever, that he was responsible for the predicament he was in. He learnt to appreciate his attachment and himself. It was a long road he was travelling on and he had barely taken the first step but he had all the time in the world to reform.

Daisy was thoroughly examined then taken to her mother who held her close and vowed never to let her go. As Daisy suckled on a breast, Maisie phoned Bear to break the news, although the police had already knocked him up to tell him. Bear wanted to go to the hospital straight away to be with his wife and daughter but Maisie managed to talk him out of it saying it wouldn't be fair on Roy to wake him up in the early hours of the morning. Bear could see the sense in what she said and finally agreed that he would pick them up and bring them home mid-morning.

After breakfast, Roy went out to play with Apache and change his water and food. He talked softly to Apache as he brushed his long black coat to make sure that it had no tangles in it then changed the bedding. Bear called out to him that it was time to collect his mother and sister, so he reluctantly went indoors after checking Apache was secure. Whilst his animal had been groomed R1 talked to ZUP2 telling him that he thought his human was doing a good job in caring for him. ZUP2 glowed with pride.

All to soon the family was back at home, together at last. Bear fussed around his wife telling her she should sit and rest then took Roy out into the kitchen to have Roy help him prepare dinner. Roy wanted sausage and mash and mushy peas and worked hard alongside his dad in the kitchen and between them they produced a creditable meal which was thoroughly appreciated.

Roy then sat on the sofa next to his mother and had the baby on his lap for a little while and the photograph taken in that moment showed his crunched-up expression.

The days and weeks seemed to fly by with Roy back at school and Bear attending college again and Maisie getting into a daily routine with Daisy.

Charlie desperately wanted to spend time with R1 but found it difficult in those first few weeks of Daisy coming home. Bear had taken on the responsibility of giving the night feed to Daisy in order for Maisie to get a good night's sleep so Charlie couldn't leave his human for any length of time.

Once Daisy began to sleep through the night Charlie managed to snatch a half hour here and there to talk to R1 who opened his eyes to many things that he hadn't even thought of before they went their separate ways to seminars. R1 didn't attend the seminars that Charlie and the other shadows attended but instead spent his unattached time learning about how he could promote the well-being of the animal he was assigned to as well as learning about the needs of other animals. He told Charlie that many humans thought of animals as less worthy than they were and were only put on earth for humans to plunder.

During one of the quiet times R1 told Charlie that if he never did anything else in his life he was fulfilled. Charlie had to work hard not to be jealous of R1 and told himself that he was happy with how his human was developing and realised that indeed he was. His human was turning out to be a caring thoughtful person and it made him realise that they both had come a long way from where they had been not too many years before.

R1 told Charlie that a large part of a shadow's role was to put their human in touch with the spiritual part of themselves. Charlie asked R1 how he could possibly do that and R1 simply laughed and told him that he would have to find out for himself, he had given Charlie a key now it was up to Charlie to find and open the door.

Charlie shared the information he had got from R1 with R45N and RZ2R. ZUP2 remained attached to Daisy for her first few months as he had had a frightful scare and didn't want to risk anything happening to his human. He had been frightened out of his wits when the S.A.S. had turned up at the squat and taken charge and had kept quiet although he was really impressed with the efficient way they coped with everything. He wondered if he could ever become a part of the squad and how he could go about it. Charlie had laughed when ZUP2 had told him this then realised that ZUP2 was serious, he really did want to join the S.A.S. Charlie told him that he had no idea how any shadow became a member of the squad but he would try and find out. Most shadows knew of the existence of the S.A.S squad but he had never met a shadow who wanted to join up before and had no idea where to start.

Bear took Roy out to the pet shop to get a companion for Apache as R1 had told Charlie that it was unkind to keep the rabbit on his own no matter how well he was looked after. Charlie had, over a few weeks managed to convey this fact to Bear who suddenly remembered that he had recently made a promise to his son. Once in the pet shop, Roy couldn't decide but, in the end, chose a beautiful white Rex rabbit which he decided to name Legless.

Chapter 13 — Meanings

Charlie, R45N and RZ2R were sitting having a discussion about what R1 had meant when he said that humans should be put in touch with the spiritual side of themselves.

"What did he mean get in touch with the spiritual side of themselves, I didn't know that humans had a spiritual side to themselves," RZ2R said, "I thought that they were just humans."

"Humans are not just humans though are they, things would be so much easier if they were."

"What do you mean?"

"Well we've found out that shadows have the capacity to be good or bad or float somewhere in between, and that although they are all classified the same as human beings, each one of them through their experiences is unique."

"I think that being a human is complicated, I'm glad I'm a shadow."

Charlie said, "When my human goes to church quite often there is a sermon about souls going to the kingdom of heaven."

"That's the place where humans go to when they don't need their body any more."

"So when they don't need their bodies any more they become souls then!"

"I think so."

"Do all humans go to the kingdom of heaven?"

"I don't know. I think so."

"What? Even the bad ones?"

"I don't know."

"The bad ones go to that place called hell; every shadow knows that!"

"Well I didn't."

"The question is, have they got to get in touch with their spiritual side before they go there or do they get in touch with it when they get there?"

"That's two questions!"

RZ2R said, "I'll tell you something else confusing. Humans are told they are all children of God!"

"Well, what's confusing about that?"

"Some of the humans that go to places of worship are grown-ups, not children!" Nobody knew how to answer that, so nobody did and for a while there was silence.

R45N said, "I think that their spiritual side is inside them."

Charlie nodded in agreement then said, "I agree. Look, if we can't see the spiritual side, it must be hidden inside them."

"If it's hidden inside them it must be hidden for a reason," RZ2R said meaningfully, "I think we should leave well alone and not go digging around."

"If we do find it, how do we know it's what we are looking for," said R45N, "I mean we haven't got the faintest idea what we are looking for! It could be staring us in the face and we wouldn't know it."

"I think it has something to do with love," said Charlie.

"Love!" said R45N.

"Yes," said Charlie "Love is hidden inside humans, I mean you can't see it can you but humans tell each other that they love each other quite a lot."

"So when they tell each other they love each other, what happens?"

Charlie shrugged, "Lots of different things, you must have seen it. It's confusing because it is not often that they have the same reactions when someone tells them they love them."

"Reactions like what!" said R45N.

"Sometimes they do that human kissing thing and sometimes they say they don't think it's true or they can have an argument and fight."

"It doesn't sound as if it is what we are looking for I mean if it causes people to fight each other."

"Not all humans fight each other."

"I wonder what it would be like to be the shadow of someone who kills someone else," mused R45N.

"I think we've gone off track here, we were talking about love."

"Is love like the respect that some of us shadows feel for their humans?"

"Partly I think, it has to do with feelings, emotions and stuff."

"So spirituality has to do with feelings!"

"It could be though we don't know what spirituality means do we. I think we should keep an open mind till we find out, after all, we don't know if it is a good thing or a bad thing, do we?"

"I don't think R1 would tell us if it was a bad thing, I think that what we are looking for is a very good thing," Charlie said purposefully. "We need to have faith in what he said."

"That's it, that's it. Faith," said R45N. "That's what R1 was talking about."

"Well I think that if he meant to say faith, he would have said faith and he didn't," said RZ2R. "And what is faith anyway?"

Charlie said, "Faith is believing in something."

"So what has believing in something got to do with spirituality then?"

"Look," said RZ2R, "I think we are going off track again, I've got a bit confused. One minute we are talking about love and now we are talking about faith. What has love got to do with being spiritual or faith if it comes to that?"

Charlie responded, "Perhaps the three are connected somehow, I mean they are all hidden inside humans, aren't they!"

The trio sat quietly for a while pondering over things they had said. Humans were complicated enough as it was and now they had to find out how to help them be spiritual when they had not the slightest idea of what being spiritual meant!

"It's never covered in seminars; I mean I've never been to a seminar where it was taught," R45N corrected himself.

"Do you think it's important?" said RZ2R.

"Yes, I do. I think R1 was trying to help us when he said it and it's up to us to find out about it."

"Do you think we should ask the teachers who give the seminars. Not in front of the whole class of course but we could wait until the end of one of the seminars and then ask."

"That's it," exploded R45N. "We should ask the P.A.T.H. squad."

"P.A.T.H. squad, never heard of them," RZ2R said.

"It's the Progress Attained Through Humility squad. I've not heard about them in years but I bet we are on the right track."

"What has humility got to do with spirituality?" asked R45N to no one in particular.

Charlie said, "I bet it has got a lot to do with spirituality. I mean I don't know how but my gutless feeling tells me we are on the right track."

"Ok then, how do we get in touch with this 'P.A.T.H' squad?"

Nobody answered as nobody knew and in the end their discussion turned to the S.A.S and baby Daisy before they returned to attach themselves to their stirring humans who were about to start a new day.

Roy was not in his bed when Bear went to get him dressed for school and he had a few moments of panic with wild imaginings before he found him fast asleep in the rabbit's pen. He looked gorgeous and Bear took a photograph of him before waking him and taking him indoors to get ready. Bear had no idea how long Roy had been in with his rabbits and made a mental note to double check that he removed the key from the back door after he had locked it at night so Roy wouldn't do it again.

Maisie was going to take Daisy to the clinic for her vaccinations and said she could handle it on her own so Bear took Roy to school and continued on to college.

Bear had decided that he wanted to be a teacher and asked his tutors what they thought of the idea and if he had any chance at all of getting into university to study and was relieved when his tutors gave him their full support and talked through the process of applying.

Little innocent Daisy sat quite happily on her mother's lap at the clinic until the injection was given then her face changed and her mouth became a downturned U as she expressed her feelings. She continued to protest all the way home and only finally settled when she suckled her mother's breast. Maisie felt guilty although she knew that having the injection was for the best. As she looked down into her daughter's contented face as she suckled, snoozed and suckled herself to sleep she was overwhelmed with the tremendous feeling of love.

Roy rushed in from school full of the day's events. A policeman had gone into the school to talk to the children and Roy was really taken with the uniform and had spent most of his time thinking about it rather than listening to what the policeman had said. He told his mum all about it from the shiny shoes to the shiny buttons before he went upstairs to change from his school uniform and put on casual clothes so that he could go and see to his rabbits.

That evening after tea, Bear took Daisy upstairs to give her a bath with Roy's help then settled her in her cot before giving Roy a bath and reading him a bedtime story. Roy informed him that he was glad that he was not a girl before cuddling himself down to sleep and Bear smiled and kissed his forehead before going downstairs to sit quietly with his wife.

Maisie said, "We need to think about getting Daisy christened."

"Why is that then?" answered Bear.

"It's the done thing," said Maisie. "We will have to choose people to be godparents."

"I don't know anybody," said Bear.

"Of course you do silly, there is bound to be someone at the college who would be willing."

"All right then, I'll ask."

"Have you checked the rabbits to see if Roy is looking after them properly?"

"Not today I haven't but he's been really caring and every time I see him going out there, he's armed with cabbage or carrots.

"Better make sure that Roy doesn't over feed them."

Bear kissed her and said he would check the following day and the pair settled comfortably into each other's company until it was time to go up to bed.

Charlie had expected to have long conversations with the rabbits' shadows but he rarely saw them when unattached and though he tried hard to start up conversations with them he only managed a word or two now and then. This wasn't what he had expected with having two animal shadows in the house, he mentally had had long conversations with them where he had struck up a strong bond and they had told him everything he needed to know in order to achieve his ambition of becoming an animal shadow but the reality was different. It wasn't as if they acted like they were superior or anything in fact the few words he managed to have with them were cordial, it was just that they were so dedicated, yes, that was it, they were dedicated. Not only did they respect their animal they loved them, heart and soul.

Charlie thought about his human, did he love him heart and soul! He had to be honest and the answer was no, not really although he had grown quite fond of him and had begun to be astonished at the things his human was capable of.

Charlie sat quietly by himself to do some serious thinking. He liked being with the other shadows but sometimes they got in his face too much with their own thoughts and ideas. He reasoned that if he listened to them and copied what they were doing he would never be able to think his own thoughts or find out what he was capable of helping his human to achieve.

He knew that humans wore out their bodies by getting old but he wondered why they did that as shadows didn't have that problem. He also knew that humans shed their bodies like a snake skin when they died but what happened to them then, what happened to the bit that had animated the bodies! Some humans, because they had not done enough when they had a chance, became shadows again like he had but where did the others go to? Were the shadows on the right track in thinking they went to the kingdom of heaven or hell?

Charlie realised that if he had behaved himself when he was human, he would not find himself in the predicament he was in at the moment because he would be where the humans who died went.

He floated through the silent house then drifted up onto the roof and watched the night life come into being. A large barn owl came and shared the roof with him and stared at him without blinking before twisting its head around to follow the activity of bats and other nocturnal creatures. The barn owl's shadow was quite talkative, and Charlie asked him what it was like to fly. The barn owl's shadow said that the barn owl didn't really need a shadow at night but he liked to remain attached as he had an opportunity to experience what it was like to fly even though it was pitch black. It was really exciting but also really scary. He said that if he never experienced anything else he would be fulfilled. He said that when he was a shadow, he was always looking for more opportunities for his human to experience life but since becoming the shadow of a barn owl he felt he had reached the pinnacle of existence.

The barn owl took off and Charlie watched it glide silently through the night and out of sight feeling happy for the attached shadow if not a little envious. He thought of 37 and wondered how he was and what he was doing then suddenly laughed at himself. He knew humans worried about humans but shadows worrying about shadows, come on Charlie, get a grip.

He noticed a human person running on the streets below him as if his life depended on it as indeed it did as a car squealed around the corner and drove after the runner. Charlie floated down to watch and saw the occupants of the car tip out of it and give chase on foot beside the embankment. He saw a scuffle, heard shouts then a loud splash then a heavy silence. Charlie moved amongst the chasers who were leaning over a parapet and staring into the fast-flowing river. He watched them laughing then saw them stroll back towards the waiting car they had not long since burst out of, its headlights cutting into the black of the night. There was no sign of the human that they had been chasing, nor was there a sign of his shadow!

Charlie was watching them leave when suddenly he felt himself being watched and turning, he was surprised to see 4Z9 close by him. He greeted him with a smile then stopped as he saw his stern countenance. 4Z9 asked him what he had seen and told him to include every little detail and Charlie did just that and told him everything even down to the type of car that had been used and its number plate as he felt intimidated by 4Z9's demeanour.

4Z9 then told Charlie to stick with him and took off following the course of the river and searching its banks as he went yelling at Charlie to look for the human body that he had heard fall into the river. It must have only taken about twenty minutes before they discovered the body but to Charlie the time flew by and he was more than a little disappointed when they found the body. Charlie noticed that the body didn't have a shadow attached and informed 4Z9 of this fact. If 4Z9 heard him he didn't give any reaction and instead pinpointed their location and before long they were surrounded by members of the S.A.S. who had used the vibration 4Z9 emitted to find them. Charlie forgot how many times he had to repeat his story to the S.A.S. but eventually he was allowed to leave. He tried to speak up for 4Z9 but was ushered away and his final sight of 4Z9 was of him being surrounded by the S.A.S.

Charlie had no time to think over what had happened as his human was stirring. Daisy was teething and decided that the whole world should share her discomfort but stopped as soon as her mother appeared. Roy was not in his bed again as Bear had forgotten to take the key out of the back door. Bear laughed as he brushed straw off of his son's pyjamas and out of his hair then took him indoors to get him ready for school.

Today was the day that Bear had arranged a treat for Maisie to show her that he loved her and really appreciated the hard work she did for the family. He had taken a day off of college and after he had dropped Roy off at school he returned home and sent Masie off in a taxi to have a massage and a manicure. Maisie had protested at first saying she only did what every mother did but at last she agreed and gave Bear and Daisy a cheery wave as the taxi departed.

Daisy started to grizzle as soon as the taxi had turned the corner and set the pattern for the rest of the time Bear was with her. Daisy didn't want to be held but didn't want to be put down and fought tooth and nail not to go in the push chair when Bear went to collect Roy from school. Bear was nearly pulling his hair out by the time Maisie returned looking happy and relaxed. As soon as Daisy saw her mother the sun came out and Daisy was all smiles and wanted cuddles as she reached for her mother.

Bear had planned to prepare the dinner for the family and do some of the housework whilst Daisy slept but, because she hadn't settled his plan had come to nothing. He watched his daughter sitting in her high chair and eating her dinner and acting as if butter wouldn't melt in her mouth and laughed, relieved that Maisie was there. He was exhausted and relieved when the evening came and he could settle down on the sofa beside his wife and doze through a programme he wanted to watch.

R45N, ZUP2 and RZ2R called to Charlie to join them as they left for their seminars but Charlie said he would be along later, so they left without him. When all was quiet, he floated up to the roof and watched everything that was going on around him. He thought back to the previous night which seemed so long ago and went over the episode in his head and came up with more questions like 'why did 4Z9 want to find the body in the water'? 'Why did he respond to 4Z9's request to help him when he knew from past experience that he was a rogue shadow'? and the one that was in the forefront of his mind 'had he let 4Z9 down by leaving him with the S.A.S.'?

Try as he might Charlie couldn't come up with a reasonable or what he thought sensible answer to any of the questions he asked himself and he knew that even if he answered the questions more questions would take their place. He briefly thought that the shadow of the human who fell or was thrown into the water might be a friend of 4Z9 but that didn't make sense as the shadow would have detached himself as soon as his human died and would have been seen by him or 4Z9. Shadows can't drown, so where had he gone? The thought came to him that perhaps he had been one of those humans who didn't have a shadow anyway!

Still muddling things over in his head, Charlie went off to the seminars and joined one mid-way through that was asking the question. "What is the importance of astral travelling?" Charlie perked up as he listened to the seminar as a whole new vista of knowledge was opened up to him.

Shadows didn't astral travel he knew but humans did, or he corrected himself, some humans did. Why, he wondered, were some humans able to astral travel and some humans weren't? Was astral travelling important to humans, did they have to experience it in order to get better at being human, was it a key to being spiritual?

Charlie waited until the seminar had finished and asked the teacher if he could answer some questions the seminar had raised as he wanted to make sure that if astral travelling was an essential skill that all humans had to acquire before they could become spiritual then he wanted to make sure that his human benefitted from it.

He was totally unsatisfied with the answer he received: that some humans were able to astral travel, some humans learnt how to astral travel and many more humans didn't as they had no idea that they could. The teacher told him that the word 'astral' meant, as near as it could be interpreted 'coming from the stars.'

The teacher left Charlie ruminating over what he had said but being no nearer to answering his question. Charlie felt frustrated with his inability to find answers to his questions and time passed before he realised that he had left his human to stumble through his morning routine by himself.

He attached himself to his human in the middle of an argument as Maisie was asking him what on earth was the matter with him. Charlie had to work hard to activate his human to give the proper responses and get him back on track and, for a time at least, was happy not to have so many questions weighing him down.

Chapter 14 — I-spy

4Z9 watched Charlie leave the waterfront then watched the S.A.S. as they worked to bring the body of the drowned human to human attention until he was vacuumed up and ejected into a vacuum container at headquarters for a month before being transported to a different nondescript statue in the suburbs of a major city where the only life forms who showed any interest in it were pigeons. 4Z9 had had plenty of time to think whilst in the container which was all he could do as being in a vacuum prevented him from moving. He had worked undercover with the S.A.S. the whole of his existence and had infiltrated many shady shadow organizations without blowing his cover which was essential if he was to continue his work. There were only two shadows who knew of his undercover role and it was imperative that he didn't blow his cover. Being held for a month was of no consequence to him as it gave him valuable thinking time.

4Z9 knew Charlie from when he had been a gang leader and hadn't been impressed by him or any of the shadows in his gang, he thought of them as small fry, none of them were big time trouble makers and he had no problem manipulating them to his will. 4Z9 had used the gang as a mantle to build up a reputation of being clever, cunning and ruthless and he had achieved it and had gained access to serious shadow organizations.

The fact that he had managed to escape from being sentenced to a still life statue had done his reputation a lot of good in the bad circles but he realised that he could be discovered and erased at any moment.

4Z9 had seen many shadows erased and had thought at the time that they were wiped out of existence once and for all. He thought it strange that even with the threat of erasure hanging over their heads there were still many shadows who pushed boundaries and didn't seem to care one way or the other.

4Z9 hadn't realised that shadows couldn't be erased until he had moved up to the higher echelon of the S.A.S. He discovered that the shadows who were supposedly erased were syphoned to a holding bay for a certain amount of time before eventually being reprogrammed and reassigned to a human.

At the moment he was on the trail of a shadow or shadows, he wasn't sure, in the S.A.S. who had infiltrated them but he dared not inform any of the S.A.S. as he had no idea as to the identity of the infiltrator. It was small things that niggled at him and had accumulated to a suspicion that there was at least one spy in the camp but he had to work on his own and make sure he didn't make anyone suspicious and this took time.

The majority of the S.A.S. team had no idea of 4Z9's attachment to them and simply thought of him as a trouble maker who had to be made accountable for his actions as an example to other shadows who were contemplating becoming part of the bad life.

First of all, 4Z9 needed to work out how to escape from his still life then he had to track down the shadow of the human who had drowned as he was satisfied from all he had heard that the shadow hadn't been attached to his human when Charlie had seen him running through the streets. He desperately needed to check the shadow files so that he had a chance of identifying the shadow he was looking for but couldn't risk it.

When the humans of shadows died the shadows were automatically drawn in for a debrief and an assessment before being reassigned. 4Z9 knew the system inside out and knew that although it was not perfect it would have to do until a better system was put in its place. The shadows of humans though never died, never got old or worn out and some used their experiences through their many human life times for good and some for evil.

All right, first things first, 4Z9 thought. He needed to stay low for a while and use the time to get his thoughts in order for he knew that once he had escaped, he would be flagged up on the wanted list and would have no time to think things through. He thought back to the vacuum container he had been held in and shuddered, there had been thousands of such containers where he was kept some of which held shadows that had been contained for thousands of years. He wondered what they had done to have such an awful sentence, surely it would have been better to have them wiped out of existence altogether than simply filing them away. What on earth could be achieved by keeping them!

4Z9 was pleased to have time to himself where he could think although he knew that he would constantly be checked up on. He had come to the conclusion that some humans were being manipulated by some of the shadows and it had something to do with the vacuum containers. It was incredible and he hardly believed it was possible but all the tiny bits of evidence he had collated supported his suspicions. Now all he had to do was bring it to light without implicating himself. Better said than done, he thought.

It was Daisy's first birthday and all the stops had been pulled out to make it a day to remember. There were birthday cards everywhere, even some from the hospital, and she sat in the middle of them chuckling delightedly as she waved or threw them about. She wasn't in the least bit interested in any of her presents, screwed up wrapping paper or the cards would do just fine. Bear beamed down at his daughter then put his coat on and took Roy up to a museum in the city whilst Maisie introduced the mothers with babies of a similar age to Daisy.

Roy loved the history museum and the science museum but most of all he loved having his daddy to himself. Bear bought him an I-spy book and they wandered around the streets searching for things to tick off in the book.

Charlie was enjoying the trip out also and was looking forward to a journey on the underground network when he suddenly stopped and stared causing his human to trip over his feet but luckily not enough to fall. Charlie quickly made sure his human was all right then concentrated on his human's well-being, he didn't want his inattention to cause his human injury or confusion. Once they were seated on the underground train, Charlie allowed himself to think about what he had seen. 4Z9. He'd seen 4Z9. What on earth was he doing in the suburbs!

Later that night, after their humans had settled, Charlie told the other shadows that he had seen 4Z9 in the suburbs of the city. The other shadows listened but were not in the least impressed as they had never met 4Z9 and had only heard of him through Charlie. They were far more interested in the days when Charlie was a rogue shadow but Charlie clammed up, those days were long since passed and nothing to be proud of. He resisted pressure to open up and, in the end, floated off to his classes thinking about the changes that were taking place in him. Once upon a time he would have liked nothing better than to be the centre of attention as he told of his previous exploits but now, he realised that they had been nothing but hot air.

Charlie suddenly changed his mind about going to the seminars and instead took himself off to the suburb where he had seen 4Z9 and found him straight away. He stood well back and watched him for a little while then noticed that he was not the only shadow who was watching 4Z9. He drew back into the trunk of a nearby tree and chatted for a while with the tree's shadow before returning his attention to the shadow who was watching 4Z9. The shadow looked vaguely familiar but Charlie couldn't place him straight away then he had it, the last time he had seen that shadow was over a year ago in human time when Daisy had been taken, he was looking at the shadow of FLR2, he was sure of it. FLR2 was the seedy little shadow that had approached him to tell him he knew where the Daisy was. Now, the question was, what on earth was FLR2 doing on a stake out, for Charlie was sure that was what he was seeing. Someone wanted to keep an eye on 4Z9 and had seconded FLR2 to do their dirty work. Charlie reasoned that it couldn't be anyone important who was using FLR2 as a spy as he was only given the jobs that other low life shadows refused!

Charlie spoke to the shadow of the tree and asked him, very politely, if he had noticed any recent activity nearby. The tree shadow did not seem in the least surprised by his question and told him that sometimes 4Z9 was watched by two or more shadows. He said that it was only during the winter months when his tree was resting that he was able to look around him to see what was going on for at other times he was far too busy making sure his tree could suction up an adequate water supply to ensure skyward growth and make sure the roots could work their way around or through underground obstacles. The shadow said that a lot of insect life depended on his getting things right but he wouldn't change his position for anything. He showed Charlie how he dealt with the pollution caused by humans as he shed some of his tree bark and Charlie was amazed when he learnt how trees absorbed carbon dioxide. There was a moment's pause then the tree shadow said that if he could change peoples' habit of surrounding single trees with concrete he would be much happier, after all, most trees needed to be with trees, it was wrong to make them isolated and many trees were unhappy.

Charlie offered his name and courteously asked for the tree shadow's name and was told that it was YEW2. He then thanked YEW2 and asked if he could visit again and was told that it would be acceptable although not in the spring, summer or autumn as he would be very busy.

Charlie then turned his attention to where FLR2 had been but failed to see him but didn't spot any other shadow watching 4Z9 either. He left YEW2 and floated quietly home unaware that he was being followed as he was too intent on his thoughts. He had been worried at leaving 4Z9 when the S.A.S. surrounded him and now he wondered what it was that 4Z9 had got himself into that he demanded the attention of being shadowed. Part of him wanted to leave well alone and part of him wanted to investigate. He quite liked the quiet life, helping his human and his family fulfil their destinies, keeping his head down and his nose out of trouble but he realised that there was still a part of him that longed for the excitement of the unknown. True he had done nothing to be proud of in his earlier life but he had had excitement and he craved it again.

4Z9 knew he was being watched and acted accordingly giving nothing away, he would make his move when he was good and ready, when he was sure of success so until that moment, he acted like a shadow who had learnt his lesson and wanted to atone for his misdemeanours. He had seen Charlie go by and had had to smile when the human Charlie was attached to suddenly tripped up because Charlie had seen him, he was sure, and had lost concentration for a moment.

He had also observed FLR2 observing him and immediately felt he knew him from somewhere. He hadn't been one of his gang members he was sure and thought that perhaps he was the insipid type of shadow who stalked the fringes of groups never being considered good enough to become a gang member but useful as an 'errand boy' every now and then. The thought dropped into his mind that being on the fringes would be a great cover as it would put FLR2 in the position of observing or hearing a lot of underhand goings on, then he laughed at himself thinking he must be scrapping the bottom of the barrel if he thought FLR2, the seedy little creep, was capable of masterminding anything. He was no more than a waste of space and 4Z9 dismissed him from his mind.

FLR2 was made up, here he was getting to the top of his game and nobody suspected a thing, to them he was just a non-descript shadow bowing and scrapping an existence on the fringes of the underworld who liked nothing better than to be noticed now and again and to run errands.

He had made it painfully obvious that he was no use at surveillance work as he tried to hide himself in plain sight, making sure that 4Z9 could see him but acting as if unaware of the fact. He saw Charlie passing and thought that his doing so was more than a coincidence as he knew that Charlie had at one time, been a rogue gang member in 4Z9's outfit. He didn't believe in coincidences and decided that Charlie and 4Z9 had arranged to meet up although he had not observed any interaction between them. He would have to keep tabs on Charlie after all he didn't want his plans disrupted.

FLR2 had everything he needed and more power than he knew what to do with and, every now and then, he let his dark side get the better of him and he would simply erase random shadows on a whim, he just couldn't help himself. Some of the shadows deserved to be erased but not all of them, some were shadows who had worked hard for their humans all of their lives not that he cared one iota, more fool them he thought.

Watching the humans of shadows he had erased fall from grace brought him a lot of satisfaction as he brought them to their knees. Most of them scrapped an existence on the fringes of their society, not unlike him he thought, and why should he have to suffer when he deserved so much more. He wanted recognition, admiration, shadows round him who respected him for who he was and what he was capable of but he wasn't getting any of that. Here he was the most powerful shadow on earth and nobody knew it, what good was that!

All that was about to change very soon though as he had what he thought was a master plan prepared and ready to be actioned.

FLR2 had never had any regard or respect for humans at any time in his existence, he thought them puny and easy to manipulate. He had attended many of the seminars right from the moment he came into existence but had never understood why it was that shadows worked in service to humans and not the other way round!

FLR2 admitted that he had a gift, he was able to manipulate other shadows and humans without it being obvious that he was doing so. Shadows, like humans had a failing in thinking that the weak were of no importance.

The shadow of the human Prime Minister wasn't towing the line like he should and his human was running amok when in session in Parliament or at home in Downing Street when playing host to certain dignitaries. Shadows who supported very important human people were kept separate from other shadows and carefully schooled in how to support people with power as it had been proved by the shadows that human people couldn't handle having any sort of power very well at all.

The plan was simple, he had to admit to himself, but brilliant. When the shadow of the present Prime Minister detached himself and left for higher schooling that very night he would be erased and replaced with a shadow chosen from the container prison. FLR2 had taken quite a long time to choose a replacement shadow and the one he had finally chosen of a politician from centuries ago would fit in perfectly, he was sure.

Life, he thought was very good, particularly at this moment in time when all the fruits of his endeavours seemed to be ripening. He had never known a time when he didn't want to become the top of the tree and had always worked towards it. He deliberately had chosen to become a whining whinging shadow as he found that other shadows left him alone unless they wanted something and it suited him entirely. It had taken a long time for him to get to the top of the tree and he was determined that now he was there he would stay there, no one was going to topple him like he had toppled his predecessors. He laughed as he thought of the shadows that he had erased on his way up; they had thought him worthless but he had outwitted them all. His predecessor had been a brilliant strategist who had introduced many innovations to the shadow movement, the latest being the Truth Bubbles and FLR2 was making good use of the knowledge he was collating from their use. His predecessor had also set in motion methods to highlight those shadows, apart from those in service, who had never been attached to a human at any time. FLR2 had no idea how the shadowless humans were discovered he only knew that they were. He had discovered that there were thousands of shadows without humans and was in the process of wondering how best to use the information. He also knew that 4Z9 was one of them.

He hadn't erased his predecessor he had simply absorbed him so that all the knowledge he had had transferred immediately to him. It had been quite a battle at the time as his predecessor fought against him but the suddenness and the ferocity of the attack won the day.

Feeling very pleased with himself, FLR2 floated back out onto the streets of the city and very soon found himself running errands seemingly pleased to be of service however menial the task. One day, he thought, they will all find out to their cost of thinking him worthless but at the moment he had activities to set in motion.

Chapter 15 — FLR2

FLR2 was furious and for quite some time couldn't think straight, for the unthinkable had happened and all his well-laid plans were for nothing.

For some unknown reason known only to itself the shadow of the Prime Minister hadn't detached that night which meant that the shadow from the container that he had pre-timed to let its occupant free that night to take the Prime Minister's shadow's place couldn't attach to him so instead had gone off into the night and was now listed as absent without leave.

FLR2 had returned to the streets thinking everything had gone to plan and was congratulating himself whilst busy waiting to run an errand when he overheard shadows nearby laughing and talking about a funny new shadow on the block who claimed that he had once been a shadow to the Prime Minister several hundred years ago. This was too much of a coincidence and he left for number ten and infiltrated the minds of several of the human servants then quizzed their shadows and learnt that all his planning was for nothing. He didn't believe the shadows when they told him that the Prime Minister had been ill with a stomach bug during the night, did they think he was that stupid that he would fall for such a yarn!

His fury was overwhelming, he couldn't think straight and blamed every shadow for the failure of his fool proof plan. There had to be a spy somewhere who had told the Prime Minister's shadow not to detach himself that night, there just had to be otherwise why would he choose that very night to stay attached when every other night without fail he had detached and gone to his seminars!

He took himself away from Downing Street and knowing he was not thinking straight, tried to calm down so that he could apply logic to his thinking. In spite of this effort, his emotions got the better of him and he erased hundreds of innocent shadows in the hope that he might have trapped the spy amongst them. He had no idea who the spy was. Here he was, a shadow who had shot to the top of his profession having been thwarted on a whim by the Prime Minister's shadow. The more he thought of it the more he stoked up the fire of fury.

A few days later in the House of Commons the Prime Minister said that he was setting up a Shadow Cabinet in order to make MPs accountable as he said, "The Government has to be transparent."

FLR2 was not fooled in the least and thought that he had underestimated the Prime Minister's shadow who must be very powerful indeed if he could get his human to do his will. Shadow Cabinet indeed. The irony was not lost on him but he wasn't smiling as he thought through ways of getting his plan back on track after all, he thought, he had the advantage. The Prime Minister's shadow didn't know who his adversary was or even had any idea that he was going to be replaced. FLR2 smirked as he thought that even if K04 was aware of being targeted he would never ever suspect the whinging humble little shadow FLR2 portrayed.

K04, the name of the shadow assigned to the Prime Minister would have been very surprised indeed to have known the kind of thoughts emanating from FLR2, not that he knew him or even knew of him for he very much moved in higher circles and didn't bother himself thinking of lesser shadows. Right from the very beginning of his existence he had been trained in the art of assisting powerful humans and even if he did say so himself (he did), he was very good at it. K04 had not deliberately foiled FLR2's plans by not detaching himself to go to his studies though he would have done if he had known anything about them. His human was genuinely not feeling well and was up most of the night so there was no way for K04 to leave him.

The daily paper was full of politics and Bear for one had had enough of it.

He threw the paper down and looked at his wife Maisie saying, "I'll be glad when the election is over and all the fuss dies down, flipping MP's giving all that spiel about what they are going to do then once they are in, they either support or try to snooker each other. I hate politics."

Roy chose that moment to come bursting into the kitchen crying that one of his rabbits had died and Bear took his hand, glanced over at his wife and grimaced, then went out into the garden with Roy and found the dead rabbit which looked to have died from natural causes as far as he could tell. He hugged Roy close to his chest unable to think of anything to say. The rabbit was obviously dead and all that went through his mind was where in the garden he could bury it although he didn't say as much to Roy.

Charlie sat with R1, the shadow of the dead rabbit and for the first time had a long conversation with him before he moved on. He listened attentively and learnt, for the first time, about the animal kingdom, the place where every animal came from and returned to when they died. He was told that all animals were pure and that they chose to come down to earth to help humans progress. When the shadow finally left, Charlie thought over everything he had been told, his mind full of wonder at the sacrifices that every animal made. None of them, it seemed, were safe from human exploitation. Knowing this made him feel very humble and doubled his certainty that he wanted to become a shadow to a wolf.

Charlie finally sussed that he was being followed having had several close encounters with an unknown shadow. He told R45N to check for him as he was worried that he was getting paranoid but really started to get worried when R45N confirmed his suspicions. They both then discussed what they should do about it, should they confront the shadow and ask him what his game was or should they say and do nothing except keep a watch on it.

They eventually decided to do nothing as they were not sure that they could handle a confrontation but they did inform RZ2R and ZUP2 but told them not to do anything except observe and report back to Charlie.

There was a strange expectancy in the air, it felt like everyone was holding their breath in anticipation of something happening but, for a couple of nights at least, nothing did.

On the night something did it took all the shadows by surprise even though they had been expecting something to happen. They left for the seminars as usual and found themselves in long queues outside some of the Truth Bubbles before they could attend their seminars. S.A.S. guards were there to ensure every shadow that arrived for the seminars obeyed the instruction to line up. Charlie remembered back to when he was supposed to have gone in a Truth Bubble and felt the same exasperation, what a waste of time! He wondered why some of the bubbles were not being used as from the outside of them they all looked the same. He knew that on earth a lot of human utensils and machinery wore out or broke down but it had never occurred to him that shadow objects could.

Fifty-two shadows that weren't assigned to humans were caught and vacuumed into containers but there was no evidence of any plot being hatched against important humans. A few shady dealers were uncovered but they were left to continue their dealings and when they stepped out of the bubble, they had no awareness that they had been identified.

In the early morning on returning to their humans Charlie and R45N checked that each other were all right.

"What was that all about. What is the point of telling us to line up at the Truth Bubbles if we never go in them?" offered R45N.

Charlie did not respond for a little while then said, "There's more to those Truth Bubbles than meets the eye. Why make us all queue up for nothing, it just doesn't make sense."

"Perhaps it's a form of control," ZUP2 offered.

Charlie and R45N looked at him but said nothing.

Bear finally got Roy to stop dawdling over his breakfast and took him off to school after kissing Maisie and Daisy goodbye. Roy had decided that he was all grown up now and could walk to school by himself but Bear would have none of it, although he did agree to shake hands outside the school gates instead of kissing and hugging as usual. As he watched his son walk down the path and onto the school playground, he felt very emotional, his little boy was growing up.

The BA ed course that Bear had enrolled in was very stimulating as well as being very demanding. He found it very difficult when his homework requested him to give opinions for and against something as it felt like he was arguing with himself. He managed to give his work in on time but a few times Maisie had to pull him up for being short with her or Roy but never with Daisy.

Sometimes Bear could really concentrate and stay focused on lessons then at other times he found himself floundering and unable to understand what was going on or what was required of him. If he had only known that the mixed feelings, he was having was down to Charlie and not him he may have felt better about himself but he didn't so he couldn't!

Charlie knew that he wasn't giving his human 100% and felt guilty which just added to his dilemma. He couldn't get his mind off of the Truth Bubbles and the fact that there could be more to them that met the eye. Why were they called Truth Bubbles? Charlie felt that he was getting near the truth but was pulled up by R45N who told him that if he didn't start concentrating on his human his change in behaviour would notify the authorities that something was up and as he already had someone following him things might just take a turn for the worst.

Charlie had got so used to being followed that he now took it for granted but as soon as R45N had reminded him he could see the wisdom in her words and pushed the unwanted thoughts away and focused on his human family and his course.

The same political party was returned to office much to Bear's dismay and he had a grump about it which fell on deaf ears so eventually he kept his opinions to himself. He let Roy help him build a larger run for his one remaining rabbit then they took that rabbit to the vets for his annual injection. Bear was very proud of the way his son took care of the rabbit, going out in all weathers to muck him out and give him fresh food. Bear hadn't had the benefit of looking after an animal as a child, it would have been all right when his mother was alive but after she died his heart was so full of missing her that he never got around to asking his dad. The thought of his dad brought him up short, he hadn't thought of him in a long time. He wondered if his grave would be overgrown and mentally promised his dad that he would go up to the cemetery and sort it out.

4Z9 had kept his head down all this time and had continued to act as if he had learnt his lesson and was trying to make amends but still managed to keep an ear open to the conversation of passing humans and their shadows so that he knew what was going on. He learnt about the purge on shadows without humans and felt himself lucky not to have been caught up in it. He was amazed at how much information he could glean from overheard conversations. Being attached to a still life in the city had its benefits after all.

4Z9 noticed a flurry of activity nearby and turned his attention to what might be the cause and saw a large crowd of people marching down the roads with banners or cardboard daubed with various messages and others waving flags. A large number of human police accompanied them as they made their way passed the statue where 4Z9 was standing.

"What do we want—justice, when do we want it—*now*." The protest was about homelessness and 4Z9 observed that many of the humans in the crowd didn't have shadows, in fact he was surprised at how many there were and wondered if there was a connection between homelessness and not having a shadow. He thought back to the recent purge of shadows without humans and wondered why humans didn't do the same for humans without shadows!

FLR2 still came regularly to observe him and 4Z9 began to think that there was more to FLR2 than what met the eye. The fact that FLR2 made much of trying to hide whilst standing out puzzled him, why go to all that trouble! It had been obvious that he had despised his human and had done absolutely nothing for her. 4Z9 wondered how the human girl was doing now. He knew that she would have been assigned a new shadow and hoped that she was living a good life.

As he stared after the marchers, 4Z9 became aware of a shadow standing nearby who was trying to get his attention.

"Do you want to swop places?"

The question came as a surprise but 4Z9 smelt a rat. "No, I don't."

"My human is dying in hospital and I thought that you could swop with me."

"Well I don't want to and you should be with your human."

The shadow seemed nervous and uneasy and kept glancing around. "Look, if you swop before my human dies you will then be free to do your own thing."

"I don't want to be free to do my own thing, I am where I belong until I am set free."

"But you will be free, don't you see it. Please swop with me, I need some quiet time."

"Go away," 4Z9 said and to his surprise the shadow did.

He stared around himself for a while then went back to learning all about the statue he had been attached to as if in preparation for the time when he was assessed about it before being unattached.

FLR2 was confronting the shadow B212 who had tried to get 4Z9 to swop places "Did you tell him your human was dying?"

"Yes."

"Did you point out that when the human died, he would be unattached and free to do his own thing?"

"Yes, I did, but he didn't want to swap," the shadow said miserably wishing he was somewhere else.

"Did you tell him that the shadow of the drowned human had been found and had been vacuumed?"

"No," B212 responded fearfully. "There wasn't a chance to."

"You mean you forgot the most important thing."

"No I—Yes, I—" B212 spluttered to a halt frightened beyond words.

FLR2 glanced casually around then almost as casually erased B212 thinking it was a shame that his human would be without a shadow but as the human was dying anyway there was no harm done. He thought about 4Z9 and wondered if he could be wrong about him after all he had been offered very tempting bait but had refused to bite. Since he had been in the top position of power, he could access the records of most of the shadows and he carefully perused them to highlight infiltrators laughing as he thought that he was the biggest infiltrator of them all. From the records he had learnt that 4Z9 was working as an undercover agent for the S.A.S. but try as he might he hadn't been able to flush him out to prove it and now was beginning to think that 4Z9's records had been deliberately doctored so that anyone who asked for them would be identifiable. He decided that 4Z9 was a very small fish in a very big pond and wasn't worth the effort he was putting in and that he had bigger fish to fry.

4Z9 in the meantime was thinking about FLR2 remembering that he had thought him to be an infiltrator then had dismissed the thought as ridiculous because FLR2 was creepy. He had allowed himself to be taken in by the act and hadn't seen the bigger picture until now. He had to give credit where it was due, FLR2's role play was almost perfect, almost too perfect for it allowed him to mix in circles he wouldn't otherwise have been allowed in and was party to all sorts of information. He was almost invisible, hidden in plain sight.

4Z9 knew he had to be very careful indeed as FLR2 was a very powerful and dangerous shadow. He knew that he could have been erased out by now and wondered why he hadn't been. He wondered what it felt like to be erased. True he had questioned many shadows back in the holding depot but that wasn't the same as actually experiencing it. He had to, to use the human term, set a thief to catch a thief, all he had to do was work out how to go about it.

Chapter 16 — Soup kitchen

Bear was up at the cemetery tending to the family plot which hadn't been too unkempt and overgrown considering that he had never tended to it. Maisie had bought a pot plant for him to bring and he was at the moment staring down at the grave of his parents reading the words, 'In loving memory' whilst realising that he had wasted all those years when growing up and had never really known the man that was his father. He wondered if Roy would ever be in the position he was now in and vowed to work harder to keep a strong relationship with his son so that would never happen.

Bear thought back to the man he had sometimes glimpsed at as a child before his mother had died, the man who had pulled faces and clowned around and a single tear trickled down his cheek as he wished with all his might that he could have the time back again and this time he would let his father know how much he loved him.

Bear had no idea how long he stood there holding the pot plant but he suddenly shivered and looked around him before placing the plant on the grave and saying, "I love you Dad, I love you

Mum," then turned and walked down the tree-lined path thinking that, for a cemetery, the area was remarkably pretty.

Feeling suddenly tired, he sat down on one of the many wooden benches and took time to think about how he was doing as a husband and a father. He suddenly realised how lucky he was to have a family when a lot of people didn't have anyone. He thought about the march they had been on recently to highlight the concern for the homeless people and realised that his worrying about it would make no difference at all to the plight of the people. True they had shown their colours by joining in the march but they had to put thoughts and words into action and find out the best way forward without demeaning the very people he was trying to help. Feeling a lot more positive, Bear went home with a lighter step and told Maisie his thoughts as she attended to Daisy.

True to his word, he went out the following night looking for someone to help but to his dismay, he found nobody. He knew that there were people about who needed help, after all, the papers were full of it and some of them had been on a march in the city, so how was he going to be able to help anyone if he couldn't find anyone to help. Disheartened he returned home and Maisie told him not to give up but to be careful how he approached people saying they may be homeless but they had their pride.

The following two nights, Bear went out again and on the second night came across a soup kitchen van. He waited until there was nobody queueing up then approached the vehicle and asked very awkwardly if they needed any help. To his delight they did and the following night he turned up and worked from inside the vehicle meeting all kinds of fascinating people.

Meanwhile FLR2 was bored, bored. He had amused himself for a while erasing certain shadows that he thought could cause him problems but he soon got tired of doing so as it wasn't fun any more. He had requested that the S.A.S. find the missing shadow of the former Prime Minister as well as report on the progress of the shadow of the human who had drowned and gave them a hard time when they didn't come up with any evidence. He had a feeling that they didn't respect him like he thought they should but didn't want to upset the apple cart too much. As long as they knew they were answerable to him he could settle for that. He had been through a time when he had thought to disband them but he had pushed the thought aside for he felt that he needed them for a time at least as they could run errands for him and could do any dirty work that needed to be done.

Charlie stood looking at the line of Truth Bubbles watching shadows enter and leave immediately and wondering what their purpose was. He seemed to remember that they were called something else a long time ago but he couldn't pin down the name. There was more to the Bubbles than what met the eye, he was sure but what could it be! He had a feeling that their use was a way of controlling the shadows and he didn't like the thought one bit. He just didn't know how they were doing it!

He found a seminar called 'Human homelessness' and found it very informative as he reasoned that he would be able to help his human who had begun to show compassion for humans with difficulties.

Mid-way through a sentence the tutor suddenly stopped teaching and stared off into space for a moment then began to tell them about the misuse of the Truth Bubbles which were originally brought into being so as to identify the students who were now emitting a higher vibration so that they could be channelled to be shadows for important humans such as royalty, or for animals. Charlie was astonished to learn that once inside the Bubble questions were fired at you that you could only answer truthfully and that any shadow could be in them for days, weeks or years though they would not remember the fact.

Suddenly there was a major disruption in the class and the tutor disappeared before their very eyes. The whole class, who had been hanging on to every word, were shocked into silence. A new tutor appeared and started teaching about 'Overcoming stubbornness in humans' as if nothing had happened. Many of the shadows left the seminar and Charlie was one of them and took himself back to be near his human whilst he gathered his thoughts. The tutor had been erased in front of the whole class so what she was teaching them was a forbidden subject. Charlie had never seen any shadow erased before and was upset that it had happened whilst realising that there was a powerful force somewhere out there in the nothingness that monitored what was being taught to them and he suddenly felt very small.

Something or someone didn't want them knowing about the purpose of the Truth Bubbles and the tutor who had tried to warn them all had been sacrificed. He wondered whether to inform the other shadows of the house what he had learnt and decided not to as it might make them vulnerable. He had to continue as if he had not learnt about the Bubbles and had to avoid going near them at any cost whilst he gathered his thoughts together and decided what to do next.

4Z9 decided not to leave the statue he had been assigned to as he was kept up to date on what was happening by the shadows of the pigeons and various birds and small nocturnal mammals as well as overhearing the conversations of passing humans. He decided that appearing to do nothing was the safest option. He heard about the demise of one of the tutors during a seminar and realised that the person or persons in power were going through an unstable time.

4Z9 had known about the Truth Bubbles from the time they were introduced and had been uneasy about their intended use then but had kept silent as he couldn't afford to blow his cover. Although they were manufactured for good, 4Z9 knew that any villain worth his salt could find a negative way to use them.

4Z9 had no idea how many other shadows were working undercover or if he was the only one. The tutor must have known that she was possibly signing her own death warrant when she decided to inform the students who had attended her seminar the truth behind the Bubbles. She had blown the lid off of what happened when the Bubble was entered by students and there was bound to be a lot of action to cover up what had happened and deny that the purpose of the Bubbles was to glean information that otherwise would not be known.

4Z9 decided that he had nothing but admiration for the tutor who had sacrificed herself. She had no way of knowing that shadows couldn't be erased whatever they had done. He imagined her surprise at finding she had been transported to a holding depot!

FLR2 was furious again and he made sure that every shadow nearby knew it. The thought occurred to him that if he had it his way, he would wipe all of the shadows out and start again. He stopped his rant for a moment, he could do that, not just now of course, but he could do that when the fuss had died down, not altogether of course just softly-softly, and then he would be sure of having a shadow army that would honour him, look up to him, do his bidding without question.

FLR2 imagined it happening, shadows bowing their heads wherever he went and for a while was lost in the reality of the image. He wouldn't have to pretend any further that he was a little creep scrapping a living on the outskirts of society, he would be 'Mr Big'. The tutor at the seminar had been erased in front of hundreds of students whilst delivering information that should not have been delivered but he had not erased her, nor had he sanctioned her being erased in fact he had very much wanted her alive so that he could have questioned her in the Truth Bubble. He would never know now why she had taken it upon herself to break the code of silence.

He felt his fury building up inside himself again as he thought of the possible repercussions and realised that he needed to learn to control himself. He was becoming unstable, unpredictable and he had better work to hold himself together. He couldn't go on a killing spree just yet as he needed to sort out this mess and then his time would come and every shadow would be made aware of who he was. Just a little longer he told himself, just a little longer.

Many of the shadows who had attended the seminar stayed away for a time but those that did return were made to use some of the Truth Bubbles little knowing that they had been doctored to erase certain parts of their memory. The shadows were designated specific Bubbles and although they had been warned by the tutor of how they were being used, most of them were still assimilating the information and many didn't believe it anyway, it was too incredible. Even those shadows who had understood the message in the seminar went into the Truth Bubbles as they couldn't possibly refuse without making their dissent known.

Days and weeks passed far too quickly and before long Daisy was going to school, Roy was finishing his final year in junior school, Maisie was teaching yoga and Bear was teaching in a local primary school though not the one his children attended.

Another election had been and gone but still Bear was not satisfied as although a different party had got in nothing seemed to have changed although he knew better than to grumble when at home as nobody took the slightest bit of notice of him.

Although shadows knew about human years and time their own time was vastly different. Most of the shadows were pleased that they were shadows and had no desire to become humans and if, when assessed, they showed they had done as much as they could for their humans, they would still request to remain shadows as they felt nothing but disgust at how the human body aged then rotted away when buried. They were content to remain shadows for all of their existence.

Charlie though still wanted to become the shadow of a wolf and ever since he had talked to 37, R1 and the owl shadow he had dreamed of becoming good enough to do so. He knew that wolves had an even shorter life span than humans and that some humans hunted and persecuted them for no other reason than they were wolves but this knowledge didn't deter him, he knew where his heart lay and was determined to do his utmost with whatever time his human had left... Even if he didn't achieve his goal this time around, he just knew that he would achieve it sometime, he had something to work towards. He realised that he hadn't thought about 37 recently and spent some time thinking about him and imagining his joy as he floated high above the world on prevailing winds.

Charlie hadn't returned to any seminar since he had witnessed the tutor being erased and R45N had stopped urging him to do so. She didn't know why Charlie refused to attend but guessed that it had something to do with the rumours being passed around about a tutor being erased in front of the class many human years ago. She didn't believe it for a moment or about the misuse of the Truth Bubbles.

It was surprisingly easy, when the time came, for 4Z9 to detach from the statue. A tourist had simply leant back against it to have a photograph taken and 4Z9 had simply swopped places without the human realising anything had taken place. He then spent the rest of the day with the human as he looked around to check if he was being followed then simply unattached himself when the human fell asleep and went in search of Charlie who was floating above his human as he slept and feeling very sorry for him. Charlie had no idea what if felt like to grow old then decay in death but he didn't like the idea of it at all. He decided that even if he did well in the life of this human, he wouldn't choose to become human even if he had earned the right to, if he couldn't become a wolf, he would rather remain a shadow.

Charlie had no idea how long 4Z9 was hovering nearby and was quite startled when he did so.

"Penny for them," said 4Z9 as they floated up to the rooftops and surveyed the night sky.

"I was just thinking along the lines of how glad I am not to be human," offered Charlie.

"I heard that you wanted to shadow a wolf," said 4Z9.

"I do, or rather I did," said Charlie. "But I don't think I will ever be good enough."

"There you go again, putting yourself down."

"I'm not, well. I am but I am trying to be realistic, and anyway how do you know I wanted to be a shadow to a wolf?"

4Z9 laughed then swung his arm in a big circle and suddenly a large fizzing hoop surrounded them twisting this way and that but always keeping them in the centre. "Don't be alarmed," he said. "This will keep anything we say to each other secret whilst repulsing hackers."

Charlie tried hard not to be mesmerized by the oscillating circle but found it very hard to focus on what 4Z9 was saying and only just managed to pick up on the last word that was spoken by him.

"Hackers?"

"Yes, those who snoop," responded 4Z9.

"Oh," said Charlie not being any the wiser.

"Listen, I've got a proposition for you," said 4Z9 earnestly then carried on before Charlie could say anything. "How would you like to work as an undercover agent for the S.A.S?"

Charlie couldn't believe what he was hearing.

"S.A.S?" he repeated. "What, *the* S.A.S?"

4Z9 ignored the question saying, "I need eyes and ears in the suburbs from someone I can trust."

If Charlie was pleased that he had received a compliment of sorts he didn't show it.

He had learnt a lot since the day he was a rogue shadow and felt that 4Z9 was trying to use him, so he didn't respond to him and instead just looked at him before saying, "How long have you been in the S.A.S?"

"All my life."

Despite himself Charlie was shocked and blurted out, "What, even when you were a gang leader?"

"Yes, especially then," 4Z9 said then, deciding that the truth was called for, he said, "I never thought much of you or any of the gang members back then but I feel you, more than any of the others, have changed and have become the sort of shadow who can be trusted, the sort of shadow I need to depend on."

"I can't put my human at risk," said Charlie. "Or any of the humans in my family come to that."

"That's how I was hoping you would respond. If you listen carefully to me, you won't put yourself or anyone at risk," said 4Z9 who then went on to explain what he wanted.

Charlie suddenly thought of something he had wanted to ask 4Z9 and blurted out, "You remember that time when the teacher was erased in front of all the students after she told us about the misuse of the Truth Bubbles?"

"I wasn't there but yes I heard about it."

"Well, what I want to know is why they didn't come after me."

"When you say 'they', who exactly are you talking about?"

"They, them, you know, the ones who don't want the truth known," said Charlie who knew what he wanted to say but didn't know exactly how to say it.

"Oh them," said 4Z9 then gave a half smile. "Don't worry, you are quite safe. Now getting back to the question, will you join me?"

Charlie was brim full of yes and no responses, he wanted to but he didn't, he could do it easily, he couldn't do it as it was too difficult.

Charlie told 4Z9 that he was being shadowed and had been for quite some time but 4Z9 wasn't fazed and in the end, despite his reservations Charlie agreed and 4Z9 reversed the circle he had drawn with his arm and left him alone to contemplate. 4Z9 said it was crucial that he carried on with his usual routine especially as he was being watched so Charlie took himself off to the seminars and joined in a seminar about astral travelling that he had attended a long time ago when he was searching for the answer to how shadows helped their humans become enlightened. This realignment with previous thoughts helped him to push his thoughts since his meeting with 4Z9 well into the background and concentrate on the seminar information in the hope that he could discover more about how to help his human. After the class he waylaid the tutor and asked him what being spiritual was and how best could he help his human.

The tutor was quiet for a while as he observed Charlie then said, "Being spiritual is more about promoting the essence of human beings rather than promoting the physical."

Charlie just looked at the tutor having completely been taken out of his comfort zone, what was this 'essence' that the tutor was talking about.

The tutor realised that Charlie was floundering and in a kindlier tone pitched further information at a level that Charlie could understand. "You must realise, Charlie, that even really compassionate humans have faults, not one of them, even the most seemingly pious is as pure as any animal on this earth."

Charlie wasn't shocked by this information as he had spoken to animal shadows.

"Charlie, your human is showing compassion to other humans by helping where he can without thought of being recognized or thanked. I don't think that you need to do anything other than what you are already doing. Just continue as you are but remember that it may take some humans many lifetimes to reach a spiritual state."

Charlie watched the tutor float away thoroughly downhearted at being reminded that reaching a spiritual state was going to take some humans many human lifetimes. How was he to know which human his human had reincarnated into so that he could continue to help him! He began to wish that he hadn't asked the tutor as now the tutor would be aware of his thoughts and would perhaps think that Charlie should be concentrating more on the day-to-day life of his human.

Bear continued to work at the soup kitchen and had also approached local supermarkets about either putting out a food donation box or collecting some of the perfect food that was being thrown away. Both projects were slow to take off but he stuck at it and soon saw both projects take off, especially the food donation box and he realised that there were a lot of good people out there, people who wanted to help but didn't, up till then, know how to. He was well known by the regulars now and would exchange friendly banter with some of them. He longed to just put his hand in his pocket and give out money but had refrained from doing so after being given advice from the humans who ran the soup kitchen who said that there was a fine line between offering help and being demeaning.

Maisie was three months pregnant but was in radiant good health, partially due to her popular yoga classes, and refused to listen to Bear who kept insisting she take it easy. Their kitchen was covered in drawings from Daisy and Roy who got on well most times except when Daisy got out of trouble by flashing her big blue eyes at her father, though the same action did not work with her mother.

Roy had started karate classes run in a nearby church hall and Bear had to put his hand in his pocket more than once to get karate suits and coloured belts. Maisie had been reluctant for her son to learn what she thought was a fighting art but soon relented as she saw him grow in skill and confidence. She often went to watch him during his class and was impressed by the sensei (class teacher) who said that martial arts were a means for the students to find out about the different aspects of themselves and work on them, martial arts was more about fighting inner battles than external ones.

Chapter 17 — Infiltration

Once he realised that his family was not at risk, Charlie worked hard to keep 4Z9 informed of what was happening in his local community, the soup kitchen being the place where he picked up most of the information. He was still being followed on occasion but made sure to act as if he was unaware of the fact.

4Z9 was pleased to have Charlie on side as he had got another pair of ears and eyes he could trust. He had been successful in tracking down the shadow of the human who had drowned many years ago through a process of elimination. First of all he had checked for the vibration but had found no evidence of it. He knew that there were ways to mask/change or even eliminate a vibration, so he wasn't too worried when that avenue of research came to a dead-end. It was important though that he found a new lead as the shadow in question had been working for him and he needed to find out what he has found out, if anything. When he hadn't made contacted in the usual manner, 4Z9 decided that the shadow hadn't reached him because he couldn't and the only place he could be therefore was either in the holding depot in a vacuum where shadows who had been erased ended up or the prison container depot.

4Z9 was right, he found the shadow in the erased depot and had long conversations with him to bring himself up to date before he sent him back out into the field. There was a lot of trouble from warring gangs in the big cities and it was part of 4Z9's remit to bring the shadows of the humans to heel, though this activity had been put on the back burner for the moment due to the disappearance of the chief of the shadows.

4Z9 did not think that there was a connection between the disappearance of the chief and the warring gangs but he couldn't totally discount it. To date, no shadow had shown their hand in trying to take over the organization and there were also no clues as to the chief of shadows' whereabouts though the searches for him had been rigorous. 4Z9 concluded that the only explanation for the disappearance was that the chief had been absorbed as that would explain his disappearance, but 4Z9 didn't think that there was any shadow capable of doing it. If the chief had been absorbed, then all the information he had gleaned over thousands of years would be available to the new shadow on the block.

4Z9 had also managed to track down PC1, the shadow who had claimed to be a former Prime Minister and had had many long discussions with him in an oscillating circle. The conversations had also been illuminating. PC1 had managed to remain invisible since being released from the container by ensuring that he did not give off a vibration which would make his whereabouts known, he could literally go anywhere without any organization being any the wiser, although he did have to be careful about the sudden raids that the S.A.S. were known for. PC1 informed him that FLR2 was the shadow he was looking for but 4Z9 laughed out loud, totally disbelieving that the creepy little shadow was capable of anything major. He decided that it was best to leave no stone unturned though and what he found at first surprised then alarmed him.

4Z9 began to realise just how dangerous FLR2 was and just how perfect his cover had been. He had not suspected a thing. All this time he had been looking for infiltration in the ranks and now he had proof that FLR2 was the enemy. He remembered that he had briefly suspected FLR2 many years ago but had dismissed the idea because he had been taken in by FLR2's cover. How could a feeling be offered as proof? FLR2 had been sentenced to shadow a telegraph pole in the middle of nowhere so how had he escaped and why hadn't 4Z9 picked up on the fact that he had?

It was no use berating himself about what had or hadn't happened as that would achieve nothing. 4Z9 set to work with a positive frame of mind.

There were rumours circulating amongst some shadows that the S.A.S. was going to be disbanded and 4Z9 knew that FLR2 was behind the proposed strategy. He thought that perhaps FLR2 had failed in his attempts to get the S.A.S. on side so had decided to take their thunder by ensuring the organisation was completely stripped of their power and he thought that disbanding them would achieve just that. He had no idea that they were untouchable.

The S.A.S. worked tirelessly to help the human police when bodies were discovered although the human police had no idea of their assistance. They alerted the human police by temporarily replacing some of their shadows and manipulating the humans so that they discovered the whereabouts of the body and/or any evidence and then withdrew and observed the police in an effort to see if they could improve their own policing skills. When a body that was taken to a mortuary or had no shadow they left one or two S.A.S. shadows in attendance in case the shadow did show up. Quite often though the shadow of a body that had been killed was identified immediately as their vibration changed. These shadows were erased and ended up in a holding depot to be debriefed, re-briefed then assigned to another human, who, for some reason or other, had no shadow.

FLR2 knew that the S.A.S. were looking for him but the fact didn't bother him in the slightest. They would soon learn that he also was untouchable, he had thousands of years of knowledge at his fingertips. Well, that wasn't exactly true he laughed, as he didn't have any fingertips though he did have the knowledge. He was having a problem lately with the shadow he had absorbed finding it harder and harder to keep him subdued. There was so much knowledge that he had to work through, some of it in zipped memory pockets. He reckoned that even if he was left alone for a decade, he wouldn't have made much headway. The fact that the chief kept trying to separate from him wasn't helping either!

FLR2 wished that he had tried to disrupt the S.A.S when he had thought of it even though he knew the action wouldn't have succeeded. He was sure that any attempt to target them would cause them to focus all their energies into finding who was behind the coup which would then give him the chance to carry out his masterplan whilst they were focused elsewhere.

FLR2 stopped and thought deeply for a moment realising that he had a weakness in thinking he was invincible. True, he was more powerful than any other shadow had been but without the chief he could still be erased. He didn't know why members of the S.A.S. couldn't be erased and decided that it just wasn't fair. He squirmed as he thought of it but he had to face the truth about himself, with the chief he was powerful, without the chief he was vulnerable.

FLR2 wondered why he had been designated to be a shadow to a human in the first place. It was a mystery to him and he blamed all his setbacks onto his human who had since been adopted and was living a happy life. On the one hand he was glad to be free of her but on the other he was angry that she was happy with a new family. He identified her new shadow and made sure that he knew he was being followed as well as harrying the other shadows in the household. Although it amused him for a time, he decided that he had bigger fish to fry. He didn't really have time to concentrate on her as he had major plans to consider but when they were actioned, he would return and destroy not only her life but the family she had joined!

FLR2 withdrew from the places he usually frequented and was no longer seen creeping around seeking to do menial tasks and very few shadows missed him. He had wanted to just run amuck and erase them all and had come surprisingly close to attempting to do so so great was his fury. He was furious that they were untouchable. He was the one that should be untouchable, not them!

FLR2 had noticed that since he had absorbed the chief, he had become more vengeful, his fuse had become shorter so he backed off and carefully planned his future actions. He didn't want a moment's revenge ruining his dreams and all the effort he had put in over the years. If he didn't learn to control himself, how could he control an army! If he failed, he would have nobody to blame but himself.

He came across an isolated aircraft hangar and began to form his shadow army in it. Once formed each shadow attended classes and was indoctrinated in his ideals. They had come into existence because of him and they were only there to do his bidding without question. They numbered three hundred at the moment but every day their numbers grew. When he walked amongst them, they shouted their allegiance to him and at last he felt he was getting the recognition that he so rightly deserved. He wasted a lot of valuable time parading up and down in front of them receiving their praise but he continued doing it as it made him feel good.

FLR2 had had time to think about how he wanted his shadows to behave. They had to appear to work positively with the humans they attached to so that they could infiltrate the human society without suspicion. He suspected that a time could come when some of his shadows could be questioned in the Truth Bubbles so he programmed them so that their real purpose couldn't be extracted no matter how ruthlessly they were questioned.

The time was coming when he would show the world who was boss and woe betide anyone who didn't bow down to him. He had been saying the same old thing to himself for years and he began to realise that maybe for the first time he had misgivings that maybe he was not up to the task, even with the chief inside him. He pushed the negative thoughts aside but they crept back and he knew that if he was ever going to make a move, he had better do it soon before he totally lost belief in himself. In order to promote confidence in himself he decided that it was about time he shed his FLR2 identity and instead make a name for himself as A1. He repeated his new identity a few times and began to feel a lot better about himself.

A1 decided not to make an outright attack on the S.A.S, he would just use them to do his dirty work and run menial tasks for him. The thought made him feel that he was strong, a mastermind who was powerful and untouchable. Yes, that was it, untouchable. Now he had become A1 he was untouchable!

Even though he had shed his FLR2 persona he was still having battles controlling the chief he had absorbed. For some reason the chief wouldn't stay in his background. He wondered if the chief could remerge from him then decided he wasn't thinking straight. It couldn't happen surely.

A1 decided he would just take half of his shadow troops and quietly infiltrate them into one of the suburbs and take over their humans whilst their shadows were attending seminars. There was bound to be a disruption of sorts from the returning shadows who couldn't reattach to their humans but as they all returned at different times, he was sure that his clean up squad could vacuum them up in no time. The vacuumed shadows could then swell the numbers of his army in the hangar. If everything went to plan the S.A.S. would be far too busy looking for the chief or sorting out the disruption and he could get on with his master plan! It was perfect, simply perfect. He was a genius.

Chapter 18 — Mosaic

Whilst Bear was helping out in the soup kitchen Charlie had a chance to chat to the shadows of humans who turned up for a meal although many of them did not have shadows, not because they didn't want or need them but because their designated shadow had deserted them. He still felt guilty over the way he had deserted his human all those years ago and felt that no matter how hard he tried he would never account for the time he had lost. Sometimes he wondered if all the effort he was now putting in was for nothing because he couldn't change the past but realised that he now genuinely loved and respected his human.

One day at the soup kitchen Charlie heard whispers of a shadow army being formed and listened attentively to the conversations whilst appearing not to all the time growing more and more alarmed. He knew it was only a rumour, but he worried about what would happen or what was going to happen if it was true. He duly passed the information on to 4Z9 but was disappointed when he did not get a reaction of any sort from him.

4Z9 on the other hand began firing on all cylinders and set about finding how the rumours had started and if there was any truth in them. He now knew for certain that if anything was going to happen FLR2 would be behind it. FLR2 had faded from the scene but 4Z9 had not forgotten him. Under a cloak of invisibility 4Z9 hung around various squats and bars listening to what was said. He had to be invisible as he knew that the conversations would dry up if they knew he was around. It took many weeks before he began to hear anything that he could use but once he had established that the rumour had an element of truth in it, he set about finding where the hangar was.

Roy's last rabbit died and Charlie had to say goodbye to R7 and found it incredibly difficult. He had not spent as much time with R7 as much as he would have liked to as something always seemed to get in the way but he had the deepest respect and admiration for him. R7 said that Roy had looked after his animal very well and that he would put in a good word for him with his superiors. Charlie was delighted as was RZ2R when the information was passed on to him.

Maisie was now seven months pregnant and had given up the yoga classes for the time being although she still practised the meditation. Bear had decorated the spare room with the help of Roy and Daisy who had been allowed to decorate one wall with drawings for their new brother or sister. Roy said that could he have a brother please as girls were soppy and Daisy decided that she wanted a ginger guinea pig.

One day, the whole family visited the nearby park and whilst Daisy played on the swings and Roy tried to hone his skateboarding skills, Bear opened up and told Maisie about the times he had visited the park with his mother and how much he still missed her. The floodgates opened unexpectedly and he poured out his heart to Maisie who held her silence as she held his hand. Bear wept beside her still feeling guilty about how he had misunderstood his father after his mother had died. Once he had stopped, Bear felt drained but glad to have shared his burden of guilt with his wife. The family slowly made their way home and Roy managed to get his father to agree to a take-away.

Later that evening as Bear and Maisie sat downstairs relaxing after a long day, Bear again talked about his mother but this time he didn't cry. Together they got out old photographs and Maisie remarked how much like his mother Daisy looked, which pleased him immensely.

Charlie talked to R45N before they made their way to the seminars although RZ2R and ZUP2 had already left.

"Why do humans have photographs of dead people?"

"Not all of them are dead silly. I think they have them because they change so much when they are alive," offered R45N.

"Don't you find that strange?"

"Not really, it's a human thing."

"What happens to the shadows of humans who die," ventured Charlie who knew the answer but wanted to hear it from R454N.

R45N said, "You know full well, they get debriefed, re-briefed then reassigned."

"Is that what happened to my mum's shadow?"

"Charlie, where are you going with this?"

"Looking at those old photographs has made me want to find my mum's shadow. 37 told me that she was called B4U and that she was a shadow to an oak tree."

"Why has this come up now. What's going on with you?"

"I never really thought about it before, I mean I wasn't about much then and when she died, I just didn't bother."

R45N was quiet for a time then said, "You can't continue to blame yourself for the rest of your life, sometimes you have to simply let the past go so that you can get on with what's happening now, what's happening in the present."

"I know, I know, but saying it is a lot easier than doing it."

"Do you ever think of what you might be capable of if you were free of the sack of garbage you carry around?"

"It's not garbage."

"All right then, guilt. Let the guilt go," and with that R45N left for her seminar leaving Charlie by himself trying to smooth his ruffled feathers.

Charlie left for his seminar but became aware that he was being followed again. He didn't waste time looking around he just trusted his senses and acted as if he wasn't aware of anything untoward. The feelings of being followed lasted for a couple of days and then Charlie got the shock of his life when he came face to face with a shadow who introduced itself as B4U, his mum's former shadow.

"I heard you wanted to find me," B4U said.

Charlie tried desperately to think of all the things he had wanted to say to his mother's shadow but drew a blank. In the end he muttered, "Sorry."

B4U looked at him kindly, and said, "37 kept me up to date with how you were doing. I never lost touch."

"37, what? Really?" said Charlie, surprised and pleased.

"Yes, really. Look, we will have plenty of time to catch up but I need you to pass a message on for me."

"A message! Who to?"

B4U said, "The message is that FLR2 has changed his name to A1."

"FLR2! I don't know any FLR2."

"Never mind, just pass the information on to 4Z9, he will know what it means."

"4Z9, you know 4Z9?"

"Yes, I know 4Z9, he may be our only hope."

Charlie burst out, "Only hope, what do you mean 'only hope'?"

B4U looked around then said, "Just tell him, Charlie," before moving away at speed.

Charlie watched the shadow leave, confused at how the meeting had gone between them. He had been followed by his mum's former shadow who had left a message with him to give to 4Z9. Why did B4U do that, how did the shadow know he knew 4Z9, why hadn't the shadow made contact with 4Z9 directly, or approach him before now?

Charlie kept asking himself questions he had no way of knowing the answers to and found it difficult to concentrate on his human so withdrew for a time to try to sort himself out. Unfortunately, the time he chose to withdraw was the time that Maisie started her early labour and needed her husband's support. Bear stumbled around not aware of what he was doing and being of no help at all and in the end R45N went in search of Charlie and made him return to his human.

Although the labour had started earlier than expected, it went smoothly and Maisie gave birth to another daughter who yelled the place down as soon as she arrived and made everyone aware that she was there.

Bear arrived home and paid the babysitter then told his children that they had a new sister.

Roy said, "Another girl!" before stomping up the stairs and Daisy asked what her name was and if she at least had ginger hair. Bear was stumped as he and Maisie hadn't got around to discussing names thinking they had plenty of time to do so and he also couldn't remember the colour of her hair or even if she had any!

That evening, with the baby sitter firmly ensconced again, Bear visited the hospital and cuddled his daughter who protested loudly at being taken from the breast of her mother. Maisie told him she was calling her Mosaic and waited for Bear's response. Bear told her it was an unusual but beautiful name and Maisie seemed content with his answer.

Mosaic's shadow, DRT4 made itself known to R45N and Charlie and they filled the shadow in with information about where they lived and said they would introduce it to RZ2R and ZUP2 when they met up at home the following day or so.

Later that night, Charlie was in the oscillating circle with 4Z9 who congratulated him on the arrival of a new shadow in his household before Charlie told him of his encounter with B4U and relayed the message given to him word for word. 4Z9 was quiet for a time staring off into the distance and Charlie simply focused on the flickering lights in the circle which he found mesmerizing. He had no idea how long he was in the circle but he suddenly found himself alone with no sign of 4Z9 or the circle.

Charlie glanced around then made his way to the seminars and joined RZ2R and ZUP2. Of R45N there was no sign.

He longed to tell R45N about his encounter and his new role but he didn't look forward to the inevitable reaction that he might be putting members of their family at risk, so he kept his news to himself and didn't even mention his brief meeting with his mum's shadow.

Once Maisie and Mosaic came home the family tried to settle into a routine although they soon gave up on the idea as having a routine was not in Mosaic's curriculum. She had been thrust out into a world she wanted no part of preferring to stay nice, warm and safe in her mothers' womb and she let everyone know of her disapproval. When she was six weeks old Maisie took her to the surgery to have her checked over, fearing she was in pain but she was found to be in perfect health and the doctor could not find any reason for her squalling.

DRT4 was very apologetic to the other shadows for the disruption to their humans' lives that her human was making but they all shrugged it off and said that Mosaic would soon grow out of it. Mosaic was six months old before she woke up one morning and decided that she was happy but it took the family quite a few weeks more to recover and realise that a corner had been turned.

Right from the start, Mosaic had shown she was different to her brother and sister. It had taken her six months before she realised that she was here to stay and that she had better get used to it. Maisie and Bear where worried that she never seemed to look directly at them, her head would be turned away as she looked elsewhere gurgling and chattering.

Charlie on the other hand had no such worries, he knew without a shadow of a doubt that Mosaic could see him. When he finally realised she could he was shocked as he didn't know that humans could see shadows in the shade (after all most humans didn't even notice their shadows in the light)! He had spent all of his existence being invisible to humans and now that he wasn't, to one human anyway, he felt real, he felt he had substance and he liked the feeling. He wondered if there were more special humans like Mosaic, a thought that he had never thought before. He was excited but decided he wouldn't share the discovery he had made. Supposing the other shadows laughed at him and caused him to be sent to be reprogrammed or something. He decided to only inform 4Z9 but not the other shadows as he felt he held a position of regard from them and didn't want to lose it.

4Z9 hadn't reacted to the news about A1 that Charlie had passed onto him although he was fully aware of the significance of the information. A1 was a code only used by the S.A.S. in moments of extreme peril. He had no doubt that the information he had received was genuine as he knew B4U from way back. FLR2, or A1 as he now called himself, was shoving the code into their faces like a red rag to a bull and expecting an immediate reaction but he was going to be disappointed as on the surface at least not a ripple of reaction would be detected.

4Z9 did react to the news that Charlie was sure that Mosaic could actually see shadows. Like Charlie he had never realised the possibility that humans could see them. He needed to check the information out for himself, not that he doubted Charlie, he simply realised the huge potential that Mosaic's ability could have and had to make sure for himself before he took any action.

Roy decided that he wanted to go to the local Ashton playing fields to watch a football team that could now use the field as their home ground so Bear traipsed off with his son expecting to be bored out of his mind and returned home waving a club scarf as he had signed himself and Roy up as members and was looking forward to the next home game. Maisie laughed at the transformation. She had seen her husband almost drag himself up the road to watch the game and now, in the matter of a few short hours, he was a fully-fledged signed-up member and wouldn't hear a word against his team even if they had lost the first game he had gone to.

Daisy had her heart set on a puppy and sat on her dad's lap that evening looking up at him with large soulful eyes as she worked her charms on him. Bear was feeling snowed under and looked to Maisie for help but Maisie was busy attending to Mosaic, so he was out on his own.

"Please Daddy, can we, please."

"We've only just managed to get your sister settled in," said Bear and immediately realised it was the wrong thing to say as now Daisy would blame Mosaic if they didn't get a puppy.

"Can we put Mosaic back and have a puppy instead, Daddy?" Daisy said, putting her head to one side.

Bear went to laugh but changed it to a cough and said, "Let's give it a few weeks more then we can all decided if we want to offer a puppy or a grown-up dog a home, there's lots to consider."

Daisy started to cry and Bear looked again to Maisie for help and this time she said, "Come on young lady, it's time for your bath," and whisked her daughter upstairs.

Bear watched them go then breathed out slowly, thankful that Maisie had come to his rescue and wondering where his daughter had got the idea of getting puppy from and later that night they talked over the possibility. Maisie said that she didn't want to get a puppy but was OK getting an older dog from a rescue centre if and when they decided to get one. Bear quite liked German shepherds and imagined himself strolling along with his faithful companion by his side but was told to take off his rose-coloured spectacles and get real. Bear blustered for a little while but eventually agreed that he had wanted a man dog for the image it gave him and soon they both were able to laugh about it.

When the shadows went to attend the seminars that night, they found that no seminars were taking place. They were amongst thousands of shadows milling around in confusion until Charlie decided to return to his human's house taking the rest of his shadows with him. As they floated above the rooftop, they saw groups of shadows floating about the streets and going into the houses. Charlie watched them, puzzled as to what they were up to then he suddenly knew and telling the other shadows to attach to their humans without delay he quickly reattached to Bear. The invading shadows tried to replace them but were driven off after a short intense battle. Once he was sure his humans were safe, Charlie sent out a warning to 4Z9 and the shadows still waiting for a seminar to take place. Many returning shadows found that they could not reattach to their humans although some did manage to drive the invaders out.

4Z9, Charlie and B4U tracked the unsuccessful shadows back to a disused aircraft hangar and watched in astonishment as A1 marched about shouting at the top of his voice as he admonished his 'army' for failing to do one little thing.

"One little thing, that's all I asked, just one little thing and you couldn't even do that. Replace the shadows who left their humans to go studying, not too difficult a request, is it?" A1 paused for a moment then continued, "You don't deserve to be in my army, you are worthless, all of you."

The 120 or so shadows who had managed to return to the aircraft hangar looked dejected as A1 floated amongst them. When his anger was spent A1 was surprised that he had not wiped them all out and thought that perhaps he at last was managing to control the fury that frequently engulfed him.

Charlie, 4Z9 and B4U were having a discussion in an oscillating circle after getting the S.A.S. to round up all the shadows who found they had been replaced. They then went from house to house syphoning off the invading shadows into containers so that the designated shadows could reattach to their humans.

"We've returned 117 shadows back to their humans and we saw that number, maybe more, at the aircraft hangar but we have no way of knowing how many shadows were there to start with."

"Well at least we know what A1 is planning," said B4U thoughtfully.

"Not yet we don't," said 4Z9. "I think A1 was having a dry run to see what he could achieve and was only caught out because there were no seminars held tonight. It would be a different story if there had been seminars held as you would have returned and found that your humans had been taken over. Yes, he was planning to infiltrate but there is no way he could replace every shadow, it's not feasible and just doesn't make any sort of sense."

"He didn't need to replace every shadow. He could, for example have gone into the House of Commons or something of the ilk and replaced them, can you imagine the mayhem?"

"Was that what he was trying to do when he tried to replace the Prime Minister's shadow all those years ago?"

"I wonder why the seminars were cancelled. I think we have someone on side who is looking out for us," said 4Z9 thoughtfully.

The trio finally went their separate ways and Charlie returned to his human who was just beginning to stir.

Chapter 19 — Inbuilt saboteur

A1 knew he had made a big mistake that could jeopardize all of his plans. Why oh, why, when everything was going so smoothly, was going to plan, did he spoil it, was he never going to learn. He should have waited until he had at least a thousand or so shadows under his command then he could have been successful in infiltrating the community and nobody would have been any the wiser until it was too late. He had an inbuilt saboteur he was sure of it, part of him that didn't want him to succeed but he didn't know how to deal with it.

He had another thought. Could the chief he had absorbed be the saboteur! Yes, yes it made sense to him now. Sometimes the challenge was weak and never bothered him but at other times, like now, it was so strong he had either to yield to it and give in and give up completely or fight it. Was he right, were the problems he was having due to his having absorbed the chief! He remembered that even before he had absorbed the chief, he had problems with being confident in his abilities but ousted the thought as he didn't like to remember times when he had been weak. Did other shadows lead such an up and down existence? He didn't think so. They always seemed to be the same and anyway why on earth was he comparing himself with them! He was unique, he had nobody to compare himself to. So he had moments of doubt, so what! One day, one day.

It had all been going smoothly, replacing shadows who had detached from their humans to go to seminars and quietly erasing them on their return but on this night instead of returning in dribs and drabs the shadows had returned en masse, a situation he hadn't foreseen and his army, his beloved soldiers, didn't know how to respond so had been captured.

A1 had watched the S.A.S. take some of the captured shadows into the Truth Bubbles but he knew that they would get nothing out of them as they all sang to the same song sheet and, after a time the S.A.S. must have realised that questioning them was futile as they stopped the process after only questioning a small number of the shadows. He had been banking on the S.A.S. only keying in the basic truth test and was somewhat relieved when they didn't think to delve any deeper as the stage two test would have given them more sensitive information of how the shadows would turn the humans they had been attached to to metaphorically bite the hand that fed them and turn against the state.

A1 would learn from what he perceived as an unfortunate mistake this time and not take anything for granted for that was one of the weaknesses about himself that he didn't like.

A1 wondered what was going to happen to his captured soldiers, would they be erased or would they simply be contained. If it was the latter, it would be only a matter of time before he could release them. Nodding his head at this thought, his mind turned to his immediate problem, the fact that the resident shadows had returned early because all seminars had been cancelled told him that he had an enemy, someone who was out to thwart his plans, now who on earth could it be!

Roy passed a grading in karate and earned a green belt. He proudly tied it around his middle but the new belt was stiff and stuck out in front of him. His parents took a photograph of him and Daisy said that she wanted to join the class much to Roy's horror. Daisy was like a butterfly in the fact that she flited from one thing to the next and though her parents knew that she would get fed up within a week or so Roy didn't and protested loudly until told to give it a rest.

For him her first class was a nightmare as she seemed to have a flair for martial arts, she was a natural.

Roy had to go out to the front of the class and show them a kata he had just learnt but he kept making mistakes as his little sister kept shouting, "Go on Roy," and proudly telling students close by, "He's my brother," although they already knew it.

Daisy surprised her parents by sticking to karate classes and making good progress. Her bubbly nature ensured she had lots of friends, all that is except her brother who grew really jealous of her. Bear and Maisie noticed and worked really hard ensuring that one child was not favoured more than the other but it didn't make any difference to their children's fraught relationship until the day of a competition in the local sports centre when Roy had been chosen to represent his club in kumite and Daisy had been chosen to represent them in kata. Roy reached the semi-finals of the kumite and was standing on the mat facing a junior black belt and although he was finally beaten, he put up a good show and had even been given an ippon with an *ushiro mawashi geri*. Daisy had watched her brother fighting and noticed he was bleeding from a cut above his right eye and got really upset for him and didn't want to do her kata. In that moment Roy realised her unselfishness and told her that she was the best sister and that she would win her kata competition.

Her rivals were very good and included higher grades but her performance stopped everyone talking as they knew they were witnessing something special. Daisy bowed on the mat to resounding applause and won the competition outright much to the delight of her family, her sensei and her brother.

A1 floated through the city noticing how the shadows of humans moved them so they didn't come near him and smiled, so they should. That the shadows moved their humans through fear and not through love didn't worry him in the least, any reaction at the moment was good and anyway he didn't want to be loved, for, as far as he was concerned, love was too tenuous. He didn't know anything about love but he certainly knew about fear having been in a state of it for the majority of his life.

He had only been able to release a few of his shadows held in containers after his failed attempt to infiltrate the community and still hoped to release the rest before they were relocated. He had come up with a far better plan, one so obvious he couldn't understand why he hadn't thought of it sooner. If his plan had been a meal, it would be delicious beyond words. He had always known that he was a genius, well, perhaps not always, but what mattered most was that he knew it now. It would do him no good at all to dwell on his FLR2 days although he did have to thank the S.A.S. for giving him time to learn about himself and develop skills that he never knew he had. Being sentenced to be attached to a still life form had given him the opportunity to develop new skills that he never knew he had.

A1 was slowly connecting his army with humans that for some reason or other had never had a shadow. Once reconnected his shadows were under instruction not to change the behaviour of the human until they got the signal to do so. He had a long way to go yet but he felt that this time he did have the element of surprise as long as he didn't rush things, for who would be bothered with the homeless people or people who had problems of one sort or another and lived mostly unseen and unheard of at the edges of society.

A1 knew he shouldn't become complacent no matter how good his plan was after all he remembered that there had been a march in the city a few years ago protesting about why people were homeless. It was funny how humans got up in arms about certain things sometimes then seemed to forget all about them for a while. At the moment it was one of those times when the interest was in a lull, and he was pleased it was so.

Bear was at the soup kitchen most nights now and had become trusted by the people who frequented it. Some of the members of the team had taken over collecting out of date food from the local supermarkets so giving him the opportunity of serving in the van for longer periods.

Bear was continually astonished at the fortitude of some of the people, many of them quite gifted and/or famous and although he kept his ears and eyes open he never got too familiar. For a few days now one of his regulars hadn't shown up and he had worried over whether he should ask about her or not but when, at the end of a week she had still not shown up, he decided to try to casually mention her.

"Is Cassie OK?" was all he said and, for a moment, he thought he had overstepped the mark.

"She's changed," was the only response he got.

Bear continued serving as if no words had been exchanged and before long, he made his way home on foot which gave him time to mull over what had been said. What on earth was meant by 'she's changed'? Was she ill, was she being bullied or being hounded out of the place she had chosen to live in! Charlie determined to pass on the information to 4Z9 who had told him that any information, however small, was vital in piecing things together.

Chapter 20 — Swimming

Later that night, Charlie was talking to 4Z9 of his worries about the remark made about Cassie. He told 4Z9 that perhaps he was worrying unduly but in all the time he had been helping in the soup kitchen nothing had changed. Night after night the same people turned up at roughly the same time, which was why, to him, something felt wrong when Cassie didn't turn up and he was told that she had changed.

4Z9 didn't respond to him and Charlie worried that he might be wasting his time with idle chitter chatter. He wondered about himself, wondered why he felt the need to impress 4Z9, after all, 4Z9 was a criminal, or at least he had been. He remembered some of the things that the gang used to get up to and took a deep breath thankful that he had moved on but, at the same time, yearning for the excitement and the camaraderie of that time.

4Z9 was about to leave when Charlie reminded him of Mosaic's ability of being able to see shadows. He got 4Z9's attention immediately although the information wasn't new. 4Z9 questioned him about how her ability was progressing. He wanted solid proof and not vague assumptions. Charlie was surprised at 4Z9's probing but was able to substantiate his claim, telling 4Z9 of the conversations he had had with her as well as those her shadow, DRT2 had with her.

4Z9 remembered that Charlie had mentioned Mosaic's apparent ability a long time ago but he had put it on the back burner as he thought the ability would disappear as the little girl got older. The fact that Mosaic's ability hadn't disappeared and had strengthened filled his head with possibilities. He wondered if Mosaic could see spheres, now that would be useful not only to him but the S.A.S. All shadows could see shadows but once a shadow went into a sphere, they became invisible. Spheres, (their nickname 'bubble ships'), were useful for keeping a finger on the pulse of what was happening both in the human and shadow worlds. Only a few members of the S.A.S. had the ability to see and fly them and these shadows were charged with their upkeep. All the ships had monitoring devices on them so that their position was known at all times. Recently though, one of the spheres had gone missing and its inbuilt tracking device silenced. The S.A.S. had put a high priority on recovering it but, despite their best efforts, it remained lost to them. As many of the shadows that A1 had created had been released at the same time they knew that the perpetrator was A1.

A1 had the ability to see spheres although it took him quite a while to realise that very few shadows could. He had come across the particular sphere he was in now whilst trying to rescue his shadows from the container depot and had not looked back since. Once he had got used to the flashing lights and floating objects within it and had disabled the tracking device, he rarely left the sphere. He did not feel the slightest bit of guilt at taking it and thought that owning it was no more than what he deserved.

After 4Z9 had left, Charlie was puzzled over why Mosaic's ability had caused 4Z9 so much interest. True, he himself had been surprised to learn of it but now he just accepted that that was just the way she was.

Bear decided that the family should go swimming as he thought it important that Mosaic should get used to the water as soon as possible. Roy and Daisy had been to regular swimming lessons all of their lives and were both competent swimmers. The swimming routine had been somewhat interrupted since Mosaic's arrival on the scene and Bear and Maisie were determined to make up for lost ground.

On arrival Maisie took Mosaic into the small pool whilst Bear stayed with Roy and Daisy in the big pool and watched them use the slide. He thought back to his childhood, so long ago, wishing that he could have the time when his mother had taken him swimming back again. He had never gone again after his mother had died though his father had offered to take him before he sank into the depths of despair at the loss of his wife.

Roy bombed into the water beside him causing Bear to jolt back into the moment. He spluttered and coughed and turned to tell Roy it was dangerous and stop doing it when Daisy did the same thing. Both children were told to get out of the water and change as they were in disgrace.

Later on the family sat in the park on a tartan rug having a picnic. Roy then found a quoit and he and his sister played with it whilst Bear lay down with his hands laced behind his head thinking what a wonderful world it was. He turned his head sideways and looked at Mosaic sprawled out and fast asleep beside him then up at Maisie. "Have I told you lately that I love you?"

Maisie laughed down at him, looked at the children as they played then put her arms on the ground behind her to brace herself and turned her head up towards the sunny sky as she smiled in contentment.

Mosaic woke up, rolled over and stared at her father for a while before grabbing hold of his shirt and pulling herself upright. Suddenly she was standing on her own and was obviously pleased with herself, waving her arms out as if to help keep her balance before she sat down with a thump. She then looked up into the sky and grinned and clapped her hands together though neither Maisie nor Bear could see what she was looking at. Roy and Daisy began arguing as they searched for the lost quoit and Maisie decided that it was time to call it a day, time to go home.

Later that evening when the children had settled Bear and Maisie were snuggled up on the sofa watching a repeat on the television and talking over the day and deciding where they would go on holiday. Bear suggested that they go on a camping holiday in Scotland but Maisie said that they should wait for the children to get older as looking after a toddler whilst camping was not her idea of a holiday.

The following day, Bear attended the local church and listened carefully to the sermon then put his head down as if in prayer although in reality he was trying to understand what he had heard. He left the church and walked slowly to his parents' grave and sat down by it and started to tidy it up again and spoke to his dad whilst doing so.

"Are you in heaven Dad? Are you with Mum?"

Whilst in the church Bear had heard about life everlasting but found the concept difficult to understand. How could life be everlasting? He knew in his heart of hearts that his mum was the sort of person who would go to heaven but what of his dad! His mum dying as she had had destroyed his dad, he could see that now, it wasn't his dad's fault that he had withdrawn from his son and became bitter and twisted.

Bear wondered what would happen to him if one of his parents went to heaven and the other went to hell, would he be split in two? He wished that he could have his childhood over again, wished that he had shown his dad how much he loved him, how much he needed him. Perhaps things would have turned out better if they had clung together through their distress!

Tears flowed freely down his face as he picked up handfuls of earth from the grave and clasped them to his chest as if he was hugging his father. Had his father gone to heaven? Bear rocked back and forth with pain, he had no idea of his father's belief system, whether his father believed in life after death, he didn't remember his father ever talking about such things, not that he would have listened if he had. Did you still go to heaven even if you didn't believe!

Maisie told her husband that he was depressed and should go and see a counsellor to talk about his issues with his dad. She had lain beside him night after night as he tossed and turned and talked in his sleep and had watched his mood take a downturn. Bear was embarrassed and put on a brave face insisting that he was all right, that nothing was troubling him. He had a beautiful wife and three lovely healthy children, what more could he possibly want!

Bear made an appointment with the doctor at Maisie's insistence and tried to act as if there wasn't a problem. He could talk about his father all right but the minute he mentioned his mother the tears started flowing. The doctor recommended some medication and said he would refer him to a counsellor.

His first appointment with the counsellor achieved no more than a scrimp of personal information. There was no way he was going to air his dirty linen to a complete stranger and he felt pleased with himself for not revealing why he was depressed. By the third appointment he felt more comfortable with the counsellor, he was a stranger no longer and found himself talking more and more. As the weeks progressed, he began to feel better astounded that merely talking to someone he didn't know was putting him on the road to recovery.

Charlie didn't like the medication his human took, it made him feel strange. He decided to talk to a teacher at the seminars to see what he could do about it but when he asked the teacher he was just told to 'experience it'. *A lot of good that did me,* thought Charlie as he returned to his human dreading the day ahead.

Medication and feelings don't mix, Charlie thought after a particularly emotional appointment with the counsellor. He had thought his human was making progress but at the moment he seemed to be going backwards at a fast rate of knots. In truth Charlie was feeling guilty and thoroughly ashamed of what his human was dredging up as he knew he was the cause of a lot of the problems. He knew that he should not express his feelings whilst still attached to his human but he was overwhelmed. Not only was he the main cause of his human's present problems but he was adding to them by influencing him when attached!

Bear saw the counsellor every week for nearly two years surprised at how long it was taking him to regain emotional stability. Maisie found it very difficult when Bear went on downward spirals where he questioned his worth but never doubted that he would recover.

The years rolled by and soon it was time for Mosaic to attend primary school. Daisy was in the top year of junior school and doing well in music and Roy was in the fifth year of high school. Roy loved the science lessons better than any of the other lessons and would spend hours on his laptop at home studying the periodic table and doing his homework. He told his parents that he wanted to become a forensic scientist and they were suitably impressed although they were not too sure what a forensic scientist did.

Daisy played the recorder then moved on to playing the violin as well as having a flair for playing the piano but couldn't decide which of the three she preferred so ended up playing all of them until Bear bought her a drum kit for her birthday and his little girl blossomed.

Maisie and Bear decided that the house need decorating and decided to add a soundproofed room where Daisy could practice her drumming as well as renovate the kitchen. The family moved out of the house and rented a bungalow whilst the work took place and having been used to living in a large house, they felt cramped in the bungalow as they had limited room for themselves. Roy was on edge most of the time as he found that Mosaic had a fascination for him and wouldn't leave him alone when he wanted to study.

When they finally moved back into their own house, they all breathed a sigh of relief. Daisy shut herself in the soundproofed room and practised on her drum set whilst Mosaic spent her time sliding down into the new playroom from her bedroom then clambering up the slide and repeating the action. With all their children fully occupied, Bear caught hold of Maisie and whirled her around in her new kitchen.

Mosaic started to call her dad Charlie much to his amusement and her mother's concern. She always seemed to be happily chatting away to someone they couldn't see but they thought that she would grow out of it reasoning it was just a phase she was going through. Bear and Maisie spent a lot of time discussing her and decided that they would buy a puppy to see if that altered her behaviour.

The rescue centre was packed with unwanted dogs, many of them expensive pedigree animals. It didn't make sense, why take an animal in then discard it as if it was worthless. How cruel was that! They chose a brindle bitch that was five months old but couldn't take the puppy straight away as they had to have a home check and also it was important to see if the dog liked them. They took the waggling bundle of energy for a ten-minute walk around the premises then returned every day to do the same until it was time to take the puppy home.

Mosaic and the dog became soul mates from the word go. She told her parents that she wanted the puppy to be called Shimmer, so Shimmer she became. Daisy was initially quite jealous that her younger sister had managed to get a puppy but soon got over it as she found the puppy extremely friendly and lovable. She was allowed to take Shimmer around the block for walkies whereas Mosaic was too young to do so and she felt really grown-up and proud as Shimmer dragged her around the block. Shimmer's shadow MST3, was, like Shimmer, very approachable and would spend hours explaining things and answering questions much to Charlie's delight.

Mosaic didn't like school and kicked up a fuss when taken to it. She did however like the playtime and ran around the playground and chatted to the shadows of the children out playing with her and only occasionally mixed with other children. The staff on playground duty noticed her behaviour and mentioned it to the class teacher.

When Maisie picked Mosaic up from school, she was asked to go into school the following day although she wasn't given a reason why. That evening Maisie discussed the forthcoming appointment with Bear wondering what on earth it was about. Bear simply shrugged and said it was no big deal as parents often got appointments to go into school. Maisie told him that she had never had to go in to talk about Roy or Daisy before but Bear just told her not to worry.

The form teacher told Maisie of the behaviour that Mosaic displayed in the playground and Maisie let out a sigh of relief. Her daughter had a vivid imagination, so what! She was happy and healthy and that was what mattered most surely! True she didn't like school but she wasn't the only child in the country who didn't was she!

A1 was floating about in his sphere when he noticed a human child balancing on the blue school railings and without a second thought he swooped down and scooped her up. If he had thought to frighten the child, he was very much mistaken as Mosaic simply laughed at him then started prodding the blinking lights and grabbing at the floating objects. She managed to loop the loop making A1 feel queasy whilst she screamed in delight. He realised that she could see him when she stared directly at him and said, "See-through man."

Of all the impulsive moves that A1 had ever had this one was low on the list. He began to berate himself for being impulsive then realised that the chief had made him do it. He had scooped up a human child who was now causing havoc and he momentarily didn't know what to do about it as he literally had to cling on to the sphere as it careered wildly above the school. Eventually he managed to regain control of himself and ejected Mosaic onto the school playing field before zooming off to put as much distance between himself and the child as quickly as possible.

There was a class of children doing P.E. on the school field but none of them noticed Mosaic's sudden appearance. She joined in with the class but the teacher got a class assistant to take her back into school to join her own class. Although a lot had happened to Mosaic it was no more than a few minutes from when she had been scooped up to the time she was returned to her class.

A1 was not happy with how he had responded to the human child. What on earth had he been thinking of when picking her up in the first place? He knew the answer but didn't want to face it. He had blamed the chief for making him scoop up the child but in reality, he had done it to amuse himself, to scare the living daylights out of her but not only had she not been scared she had loved the experience. She had called him see-through man so she could obviously see him, this was not good news as he thought himself and his sphere to be invisible to all humans. Here he was, the most powerful shadow of all time being thwarted by a little girl. He wondered if there were many other humans who could see shadows and whether their ability could cause him problems. It took him quite a long time to compose himself.

Chapter 21 — See-through man

When Maisie picked Mosaic up from school the class teacher called her in for a moment and showed her some of the drawings that Mosaic had created in art class that afternoon. Huge circular forms with splashes of colour inside and a shadowy shape to one side of the circle. The teacher told Maisie that when she had asked Mosaic about her picture, she had told her it was 'see-through man'.

Maisie told the teacher she thought the paintings were wonderful and showed that her daughter had an artistic flair.

Later that evening Mosaic sat in the kitchen and drew a similar picture though this time with crayons not, paint. Shimmer lay down on the floor beside her as if guarding her.

Bear leaned over his daughter's shoulder and pointed to the shadowy shape in the circle saying, "What's that honeybun?"

"See-through man," she responded, her tongue sticking out to one side of her mouth as she concentrated on her picture.

"See-through man!"

"Yes Daddy, you have a see-through man named Charlie."

Bear pointed to the shape in the picture. "Is that Charlie?"

"No silly, Charlie is your shadow."

"How do you know that Charlie is my shadow?"

Mosaic stopped what she was doing and looked at her father and said, "He told me," before resuming her drawing.

Bear was confused "Who's that then?" pointing to the shadowy figure again.

Mosaic gave a big sigh and puffed her cheeks as she blew out then said, "I told you Daddy, see-through man." Mosaic put down the crayon she was holding then added, "he shouted at me," before sliding off of the kitchen stool and running out into the garden with Shimmer.

Maisie came in that moment having been to visit her mother who had not been feeling well. Their relationship had improved quite a lot over the years as her mother seemed to have mellowed with age. Her mother was in the middle of an online foundation course with the College of Psychic Studies and the time had flown as she examined her daughter's palm and told her a few things which surprised her.

Maisie was not happy that Bear had allowed Mosaic to stay up so late and told him so in so many words before taking her coat off and going out in the garden to fetch Mosaic and taking her up to bed.

Daisy strolled into the kitchen to have some supper before going up to bed and teased her brother about having a girlfriend. Roy, who had only come down to snack on some bread pudding went bright red and told his sister to shut up before returning upstairs.

Bear stood to the side watching the interaction between his children then said to Daisy, "Ten more minutes then up to bed young lady," before fetching Shimmer's lead, to take her for a walk.

Daisy watched her father clip the lead on Shimmer and leave the house then went up the stairs and knocked quietly on her brother's door. Roy opened the door. "What?"

"Can I ask you something?"

Roy stood in his doorway staring down at his sister. "Ask away."

Daisy looked down the corridor to see if her mother was about then said, "Can I come in?"

Roy was intrigued by the secrecy and stepped back to allow Daisy in his room. She looked around the room at the large posters of rock bands then came straight to the point. "I'm being bullied at school."

"What are you telling me for," he answered then, as he saw Daisy turn to leave the room he said, "look, sit down and tell me about it."

Daisy sat down then told her brother about the girls in her school who laughed at her because she was a tomboy and telling her she was fat and ugly.

Roy looked at his sister in astonishment as she was neither fat nor ugly. Yes, she was a tomboy but he liked that about her and told her so, especially how she played drums.

"Why haven't you told Mum and Dad?" he asked.

"They told me they would get me into trouble by saying I was stealing stuff if I told anyone."

"Have you stolen anything?"

"No I haven't, I wouldn't," said Daisy as she burst into tears.

Just then there was a knock on the door and it opened without waiting for an acknowledgement. Maisie stood in the doorway and took in the scene before her. "Daisy, Daisy, what on earth is the matter?" as she went over to her daughter whilst looking at Roy.

Roy said, "Daisy has got something to tell you," as his mother sat down beside Daisy, put an arm around her and pulled Daisy towards herself.

Daisy repeated what she had told to Roy whilst her mother held her close and rocked her gently then, when Daisy had finished, Maisie guided her daughter out of Roy's room and back to her own. Once she had settled Daisy she went downstairs just as Bear came in with Shimmer who shot upstairs to be with Mosaic the second the lead was unclipped. They then spent the rest of the evening discussing Daisy and worrying what to do for the best.

The following day, Maisie went into the school after she had dropped her daughters off and asked to speak to the head teacher or, at the very least make an appointment to see her. An appointment was made for later that day and Maisie had time to work out what she wanted to say without getting upset. She was nervous about facing someone in authority, she always had been, so she wrote down what she wanted to say in case she forgot anything.

She needed not to have worried about the meeting as the head teacher spoke to her as an equal and listened very carefully to what she had to say. Maisie's voice quavered a few times as she spoke but she managed to remember everything she wanted to say without checking her notes and was relieved when the head teacher took her seriously and promised that action would be taken.

Later that night 4Z9 was talking to Charlie and B4U in the oscillating circle which was floating just above the River Thames "—and at the same time as it (the sphere) went missing over a hundred shadows were released. This is significant because they were shadows created by A1."

"So why did he take the risk of being discovered when releasing his shadows, surely he would know we would put two and two together."

B4U said, "Perhaps he wanted us to know or perhaps he hasn't had time to create more shadows. Maybe whatever he is planning is happening soon."

4Z9 nodded. "Could be. Trouble is, all we have at the moment is conjecture, we have nothing concrete to go by. We need to be on red alert whilst appearing not to be as A1 could be anywhere. We know that he was creating shadows in a disused aircraft hangar but now there is no activity there."

Charlie said "So where have they gone? They must be somewhere!"

The trio looked at each other, searching each other's faces, waiting for one of them to provide an answer. Silence ensued.

At last the summer holidays arrived and for a few weeks the family relaxed, happy to be in each other's company. Roy got himself a part-time job in a local paper shop whilst looking for full-time work and Daisy practised for hours at a time on her drum set only reluctantly coming out of the soundproofed room when Maisie insisted she should. Mosaic spent all her waking hours with Shimmer and the two of them often sat shoulder to shoulder in the garden with Mosaic chatting away and Shimmer occasionally licking her face.

Time passed, as it does, and Roy was packing his bags to go to university. Maisie clung to her son who was now much taller than she was and told him to ring every day and not forget to wash behind his ears! Bear settled for a hand shake with him then a man hug, slapping Roy on the back a few times before he let him go.

Maisie and Bear stood hand in hand in the doorway as they watched the taxi that was taking Roy to the station turn the corner of the road and out of sight. They stood there for a few minutes longer as if waiting for the taxi to reappear then turned and went indoors.

The family went to the local swimming pool and watched their daughters swimming. Daisy had been swimming for years but they were astonished at how Mosaic managed to keep up with her. Daisy said later that she had deliberately been going slow in order for Mosaic to keep up with her although her parents knew this wasn't true.

Sitting by the as yet unopened wicker basket full of picnic goodies, Daisy reminded her parents that she would soon be grading for her third stripe on her brown belt. She had stuck with the karate lessons even when her brother had given it up having discovered girls. Daisy and Mosaic then played with a quoit until it was time to open the wicker basket and sample the delights within.

Mosaic suddenly stopped eating and stood up. "Shimmer's crying, I want to go home."

Shimmer had been sleeping soundly in her basket left in the shade and had then woken and cried for Mosaic to be with her. When Mosaic didn't appear, Shimmer went into the garden and rolled and twisted on the grass before shaking herself off. She saw a sphere float across the garden in front of her and skim the boundary hedge. She raced up and down next to the hedge trying to see into the garden next door and then set to digging furiously.

A1 landed in the middle of the garden next door and floated up to the house. All the windows and doors were shut although it was a hot, sunny day, and this told him that the house was empty. It was. A1 floated through the house then went into the house next door, which was the real reason for his visit. He knew the shadow called Charlie lived there and he was curious about him. He wasn't too sure what he was looking for or what he would find but he suspected Charlie of being a spy. He had no idea where the idea had come from but once it had arrived it would not leave him. The more A1 thought about it the more he was convinced he was right; Charlie was a spy and was therefore a danger to him. As he moved through the house, he came across a dog basket and open French doors. The alarm bells rang in his head and he whisked himself away to the empty house next door and floated down the garden wishing that he hadn't left his sphere. A1 felt vulnerable when he was outside of it and though he knew he was relying on it too much it made him feel superior. Spheres only had one drawback as far as he could see, they couldn't go through the walls and into buildings like he could. He had been really surprised when he had first discovered this trait and had bounced off of quite a few buildings before this fallibility had registered with him.

All was quiet and he was beginning to think he shouldn't have curtailed his inspection just because he had seen a dog's basket. He was so busy admonishing himself as he reached his sphere when he was faced with a snarling dog. He swooped away up into the overhanging branches of next doors tree and thought he would wait for the dog to leave. He had no idea if the dog could hurt him but he did know that the dog could see him. A1 was trembling with fear and eventually took himself away and hid in a disused underground station telling himself he would go back for the sphere the following day. The dog could see him but it couldn't hurt him, surely not!

When the family returned from their day out, Mosaic ran about calling for Shimmer expecting to see her come charging towards her. There was no answering bark or scurry of activity, Shimmer was gone. Mosaic was inconsolable and Maisie sat with her on the sofa telling her everything would soon be all right as she stared up at Bear. Bear searched the house one more time then stood by the open French doors looking into the garden but could see no sign of her. He then phoned the vets who promised to inform all their branches then took the lead and went out with Daisy to search the streets and ask passers-by if they had seen a brindle Staffie.

When Bear and Maisie returned empty-handed Mosaic threw herself to the floor and wailed, utterly inconsolable. It was nearly midnight by the time her parents managed to get her and Daisy to sleep. They stood, thoroughly drained, in the bedroom doorway watching Mosaic toss and turn and mumble in her sleep then went to bed themselves though neither of them could sleep.

"She didn't run off, she would never leave Mosaic, it's like they are joined at the hip," said Maisie.

"I know," responded Bear who was feeling guilty for leaving the French doors open.

"Who would do such a thing, steal a child's dog?"

"Perhaps she got out of the garden and couldn't find her way back!"

"If she was nearby, she would have heard us calling."

Shimmer, the object of their discussion had heard the family calling for her but at the moment she was on guard in the sphere. The sphere gave her a 360-degree view of her surroundings and she could still see the shadow that had tried to enter the sphere up in the branches of the overhanging tree. When she had entered the sphere the smell of the occupant assailed her senses and her hackles rose, instinctively she knew that the occupant was an enemy. As she examined the interior, she found the faintest of traces of Mosaic having been in there.

Shimmer saw the shadow in the tree leave but stayed in position before the call of nature prompted her leaving the sphere just as daylight was lifting the edges of the night.

Charlie was in the circle with 4Z9 and B4U floating over the house where his humans resided when, upon looking down he saw Shimmer in next door's garden running alongside the boundary fence. The three shadows floated down into the garden and B4U told them that there was a sphere at the end of it. B4U went with 4Z9 to examine it whilst Charlie scooped Shimmer up and took her home to Mosaic.

Charlie watched Mosaic make herself comfy beside Mosaic and smiled then returned to see what was happening next door but try as he might, he couldn't find the sphere until B4U suddenly popped her head out of it just in front of him and scared him as her head seemed to be floating on its own above the ground. B4U guided Charlie inside the sphere and he looked about him in wonder, it was the first time in his existence that he had been inside a sphere and he found that he had not enough words to describe it. The inside was really spacious and full of flashing lights and floating objects. Charlie desperately wanted to be taken for a ride in it and almost sulked when 4Z9 insisted they leave.

When back up in the oscillating circle the three shadows discussed what to do next. They knew without a shadow of a doubt that the sphere belonged to A1 but couldn't work out why it was parked nearby without its passenger.

"He must be close; he would never leave his sphere unless he had a good reason," Charlie said as he looked around him as if to see A1 hurtling back to the sphere.

4Z9 meanwhile had sent a vibration to one of the shadows from the sphere squad to bring a tracker and remote-control unit. When he had done this, he turned to the other two shadows and said "We should never underestimate A1, after all he managed to disable the previous tracker unit in the sphere. This new unit is a microdot that will be attached to the outside of it."

Charlie said "The outside of it. Won't it come off?"

B4U and 4Z9 laughed. "No chance. It will enable us to know his whereabouts at all times."

They stayed quiet for a moment then 4Z9 said, "A1 is only able to do all these things because he is tapping into the knowledge of the chief."

B4U said, "All we have to do is wait for him to return, we don't need the microdot to track him."

"Supposing he does not come back for the sphere. We will be waiting around whilst he's off perhaps stealing another one."

4Z9 and B4U decided to wait for a while disguising themselves as leaves on the nearby tree. Charlie felt his human stirring so hurriedly left to join his human who was just throwing back the duvet and preparing to step into a new day. Mosaic suddenly burst into the room followed by Shimmer.

"Daddy, Daddy, you found her." Mosaic gave her daddy a big hug as Shimmer jumped up onto the bed and kneaded the human form beneath the duvet with her paws before jumping off and following Mosaic downstairs.

Maisie stirred then turned over to look at her husband with a puzzled look on her face. "Did I hear Shimmer? How on earth—" but she was talking to an empty room.

By the time Maisie had got herself ready and had come downstairs breakfast was well under way. Shimmer was sitting by Mosaic's stool staring up at her and Daisy was eating toast and marmalade. Maisie stopped by Shimmer.

"Where on earth did you get to young lady?" Then looking directly at Bear, said, "We had better phone the vet and tell them that we've found her, although where she got to, we'll never know."

"She was with see-through man," Mosaic offered between mouthfuls of cornflakes. Bear and Maisie looked at each other. They had had long discussions and had decided not to respond to Mosaic's comments but Daisy, not knowing of their decision, plunged straight in.

"How do you know that?"

"Charlie told me," said Mosaic sliding off of her stool and tasking her plate to the sink and dropping it in with a clatter.

"What's my shadow called then," asked Daisy who was feeling jealous that she couldn't see shadows and was looking to catch her younger sister out in a lie.

"ZUP2," said Maisie, then added, "he wants to join the S.A.S."

"Oh you're such a liar," shouted Daisy.

"I'm not, I'm not a liar," shouted Mosaic running over to the stool that Daisy was sitting on and trying to pull her off of it.

"That's quite enough of that," Maisie called over the racket. "You can apologise to each other."

"I won't," said Mosaic stamping her feet. "I am not a liar."

"Liar, liar, hairs on fire," chanted Daisy.

Mosaic stuck her tongue out at her sister. "You're ugly."

Daisy saw an opportunity to get her parents on side and immediately burst into tears. "I'm not ugly, I'm not."

The ploy worked and Maisie cuddled Daisy and told Mosaic to go up into her room and think about what she had said to her sister. Mosaic turned and left the room but instead of going up to her room she went out into the garden followed by Shimmer.

In the meantime, A1 had achieved quite a lot after spending time in the unused underground station. He felt very vulnerable without his sphere and decided that once he got back into it, he would never leave it again. That decided he floated across the city visiting all the homeless and needy hangouts and what he discovered pleased him immensely for out of thousands of humans he saw there were barely a handful without shadows. All in all he visited five major cities and found the same result in each and decided that it was time to start stage two of his plan as soon as he retrieved his sphere and threw the switch. In the meantime he became a hair on the head of the prime minister and listened in on private conversations then became a feather in the wind then a speck of dust on a window frame.

It was during one of his transformations that A1 inadvertently separated himself from the chief. He had been so busy planning, so busy thinking of other things as he transformed himself that he had completely forgotten that the chief was inside him. He screamed with rage as he saw the chief disappear like a puff of smoke. A1 suddenly felt he was FLR2 again, he felt weak and powerless. He had to get back to the sphere but supposing he couldn't find it, supposing he could only have seen spheres because of the ability of the chief! He didn't know but he had no choice. He wept and groaned as he saw all of his beautiful plans torn to shreds. With the chief back in power he would have to act quickly or forget everything.

4Z9 received a vibration informing him that the chief was free and together with B4U returned to headquarters to attend a meeting. The chief explained A1's plans and explained the intricacies of his personality having been part of him for so long. A1 had absorbed him to gain his knowledge but he hadn't realised that it was a two-way street he was going down, hadn't realised that the chief could access his knowledge! The chief told them that A1 hadn't yet accessed his many zipped memory files but that A1 did have powers such as shapeshifting which they had previously been unaware of.

A1 cautiously returned to where he had left the sphere and was overjoyed that he could see it, he wasn't totally powerless or useless. He became a seed of a dandelion and simply floated into it amazed at how easy it was to recapture it. All the time he had been away from it he had imagined he would fail to get back inside it and now he had done it, all those worries for nothing!

A1 had learnt from his previous encounter with Shimmer that anything that went inside the sphere immediately became invisible to outsiders. He cursed his stupidity of leaving the sphere open, if he had simply shut the door behind him, he would not have been in the predicament he had found himself in.

Mosaic was in the garden next door with Shimmer and they both stopped what they were doing and watched the sphere float up and away.

Very few people came to the soup wagon that evening, and the few that did, seemed edgy and unsettled. Bear could see the difference in his customers but made sure that he concentrated on what he was there for and tried not to say too much. He couldn't understand what was going on, surely people would still need food! After he had cleaned and locked up the wagon, he strolled around areas he knew some of the homeless frequented but didn't notice anything different going on.

Charlie told 4Z9 about what he had noticed as they floated around the city looking for signs of activity of any sort then moved on to another large city but again found nothing unusual happening. The trouble was that they knew what they were looking for but they did not find any evidence of any activity. They had the feeling that something was wrong but nothing was evident to support the feeling. From tracking A1's sphere movement they could see that he spent a lot of time visiting major cities but they didn't know why he did. They returned to base and examined the similarities and differences of each of the cities he had visited. The S.A.S. wanted the chief to take him in straight away but the chief thought that that would be easier said than done. They knew where he was as they had the tracker on him, they just had to be vigilant.

A1 decided that he would concentrate all his efforts on London for it was there, he thought, that he could wreak the most damage. He had spent a lot of time deliberating over Liverpool, Glasgow, Dublin and Wolverhampton but decided that he liked the raw energy these cities produced whereas he just didn't like London though he couldn't decide why he didn't. He hovered over the city then followed the path of the Thames from the Thames Barrier to Staines and back again. A1 decided that instead of being active in five cities he would concentrate on one of the capitals' bridges as he didn't want to spread himself too thinly although he argued with himself that he could go bigger if he wanted.

A1 activated the next stage in his shadow army then took the sphere up into the clouds and thought through his plan to see if it needed tweaking but could find no fault anywhere in the plan, he was a master and no mistake. He didn't need the chief; he could do anything he wanted. He would become a legend and everywhere he went shadows would bow down to him and whisper his name. For a while he was lost in the image of his success but eventually shook himself out of the reverie, he had work to do.

A1's ability to shape-shift enabled him to eavesdrop on many conversations. He thoroughly enjoyed the activity in the houses of parliament and often sat on the back benches listening avidly whilst his sphere hovered above him on the rooftops. The activity that entertained him enforced his view that humans were puny and worthless, how they ever reached agreement about anything he never knew. It was more by luck than actual planning, he was sure.

There was no place that A1 couldn't reach and he was privy to a lot of information. At the moment he was floating in a meeting in which the chief constable was discussing plans for a march to be held in London. A1 listened carefully as the proposed route was outlined. It was unbelievable, it was as if the humans were actually helping him to fulfil his plans that would lead to the biggest catastrophe the city had ever faced. This showed him that his plans were meant to be and that he would be successful.

A1 reluctantly came back into the moment to hear that the march would be in protest of the treatment of refugees. All right, that was fine, any sort of march for any cause would be fine. He left the premises and took himself to a quiet place where he could mull over what he had learnt and use it to his advantage.

Bear took Daisy with him when he went to the cemetery to tidy up the family grave. Daisy had initially protested as she wanted to play on the new drum set that she had received for her birthday but now, as she walked hand in hand with her father along the tree-lined walkway she was glad that she had her daddy to herself. On reaching the grave she used a cloth to clean then read the words on the tombstones then asked about her grandparents, what were they like and could she see photographs of them when she and her dad returned home. Bear was surprised at her interest and told her stories from his childhood that made her smile. His parents had been good people and he wanted her to know that. Bear told her that she looked a lot like his mother had when she was a child and was surprised when Daisy threw her arms around him and told him that she was glad that she looked like her grandmother.

On reaching home, Daisy found Mosaic in the soundproof room attempting to play on her new drum set and dragged her off whilst screaming at her. The drum set was sent flying as Daisy chased her sister around the room whilst Shimmer, who was not allowed in the room, barked in a frenzy outside of it and scratched at the door. Maisie thrust open the door to the room and was confronted with her daughters chasing each other around the room whilst screaming at the top of their voices.

The sudden appearance of their mother stopped the girls in their tracks and a deadly silence ensued. Maisie took a deep breath then told Mosaic to go up to her room and she would be up to see her later. Daisy then started to reconstruct her drum set whilst avoiding looking at her mother then went and sat down with her and told her side of the story. She knew that as an older sister she should set a good example to Mosaic but felt she was justified in reacting the way she had.

Mosaic was hiding under her bed and took a little persuasion to come out when Maisie went up to see her. She knew she shouldn't have touched her sister's drum set but couldn't resist the opportunity to do so whilst her sister was out.

"Come on out and stop being silly."

"Don't want to," Mosaic said defiantly.

"All right, stay there," Maisie said as she turned to leave the room.

Mosaic came out from under the bed and stood facing her mother. "I want a drum set too," she said.

"Well," said her mother, "you are going the wrong way about it. Daisy is quite upset and you are going to have to say sorry."

"No," Mosaic stated firmly.

"I beg your pardon!"

"I said no. I don't want to say sorry to Daisy because I don't feel sorry."

"Oh, why is that then?"

"I don't know."

"Supposing you had a special birthday present and Daisy played with it before you did, how would that make you feel."

"I wouldn't mind, she could have it if she wanted it."

Maisie felt that she was being boxed into a corner so told Mosaic to think about what she had done and to apologise to her sister then left the room and went downstairs.

Chapter 22 — River Thames

The tracker on A1's sphere showed that he had been going back and forth across London following the River Thames. 4Z9 had chartered his course over the last few days and wondered what A1 was up to now as he no longer seemed interested in the other four cities he had previously visited. What on earth was so interesting about the River Thames that he spent days traversing it?

Charlie suggested that he might be planning to pollute the river but 4Z9 said that it was already heavily polluted. B4U wondered why A1 had been manufacturing so many shadows and how such manufacturing tied in with the River Thames, nothing made sense.

Charlie mentioned that when he went with his human to the soup wagon a lot of the humans who didn't previously have shadows now had them. Perhaps they had got A1 wrong, perhaps A1 was trying to help humans by giving them shadows!

4Z9 said a leopard didn't change its spots and that he didn't think that A1 was being benevolent. If he was manufacturing shadows to give to humans, then he was using his shadows to manipulate the humans for some reason.

37 suddenly appeared and greeted Charlie like an old friend then turned to 4Z9 and B4U and said that some shadows of birds had told him that they had overheard that homeless people were planning to join a march for refugees that was taking place in just over a week. Banners, flags and placards were being prepared in secrecy. As soon as he had given the information, 37 disappeared leaving 4Z9 and his companions to add the information to what they already knew, or suspected, and try to make sense of it.

Shimmer was in the garden running around in circles and occasionally jumping up in the air as she barked her warning. Bear stood in the back room watching her then called her in as he was worried that the noise that she was making would upset the neighbours. Once inside, Shimmer whined and scratched at the door to the garden and Bear told her to go to her bed and lay down though he might as well of saved his breath as Shimmer ignored him.

Mosaic wandered into the back room and looked out of the window and said, "See-through man." She pointed out into the garden.

Bear pulled the curtains and told his daughter to get her breakfast.

Al floated away as soon as the dog that had caused him so much trouble was ordered into the house having thoroughly enjoyed himself at teasing it. His plans were going well though they were taking a little longer than he would have liked because some of the humans who now had shadows were resisting them. He hadn't foreseen that this could happen, puny humans were actually trying to thwart his plans, although of course they didn't know that was what they were doing.

Al had followed Bear to the soup wagon a few times and wondered if the Charlie shadow was the one upsetting his plans, after all, his human was mixing with the homeless humans! Perhaps he should erase him, that would take him away from the city for a while. He would have to think about it for having learnt that when he acted spontaneously things tended to go wrong, he was determined that this time nothing would. It made sense to him that Charlie was a spy out to get him and prevent him from achieving the status he deserved. He would watch him and deal with him when the time was right after he had dealt with his former human…

The family went to visit Maisie's mother and found her in an extraordinary good mood. The girls played in the garden whilst Bear mowed the lawn and pruned the roses. Maisie sat in the kitchen with her mother catching up on the local gossip when her mother suddenly said, "I'm going on a march this weekend."

"This weekend, it's a bank holiday!"

"So it's a bank holiday, so what!"

"You're going on a march! What march, where's it going?"

"It's a march for the homeless and we are going into the city."

Maisie looked at her mother in astonishment as her mother had never thought of anyone else but herself as long as she could remember. "I don't think that's a good idea—" she began but was cut off by her mother.

"I'm going and that's all here is to it," her mother stated firmly then said, "I'm really quite excited. I feel a bit like a rebel."

The conversation changed to the girls and the time flew by until Mosaic came in stating she was hungry. Later that evening, Maisie kissed her mother goodbye and told her to take care of herself before returning home.

When the girls were in bed Maisie told Bear about her mother going on a march for the homeless. Bear laughed at first until he realised his wife was serious then listened as she expressed her fears for her mother getting caught up in something she couldn't deal with.

Bear said, "Good for her, sounds fun."

"She is not doing it for fun, she is really concerned and wants to show support," Maisie said rather sharply.

Bear kept quiet and went out into the garden to take a deep breath. He looked up and saw bats silhouetted in the sky above him, then returned indoors.

Charlie confirmed the information that 37 had passed to them that there was going to be a march this coming weekend and thought that the planned refugee march was going to be supported by the homeless marchers as the preparation of placards suggested. 4Z9 perked up. He left Charlie to go to his classes whilst he returned to S.A.S. headquarters with B4U and had a consultation with the chief. They discussed the data received from the tracker placed on A1's sphere where it was evident that A1 was concentrating his efforts along the River Thames now seeming to have decided not to pursue his interest in the other major cities. It seemed evident that A1 was focused on London and the River Thames in particular. 4Z9 knew that A1 was going to somehow use the coming march for his own ends but couldn't work out what for or how. He wondered if his feelings were wrong and that A1 genuinely was trying to support the homeless and needy humans. Here he was chasing around trying to protect the humans when they didn't need protection.

The S.A.S. examined the proposed route for the refugee march and saw that it went to the green near the houses of parliament. Using the evidence that A1 seemed to have a particular interest in the River Thames they highlighted the fact that the nearest bridge to the proposed end of the march was Westminster Bridge. Having identified a possible target they then were left with many possibilities as to what A1 intended, what was to be the climax of the march. Surely it would not be as simple as to crowd the bridge and bring traffic to a halt!

4Z9 reflected on the information held to date. A1 had initially shown interest in five cities then had concentrated on one, London. He decided to act as if A1 was going to cause a catastrophe. If the S.A.S. were on hand at least there would be no harm done if the proposed march really was just that, a march and there was no need to take any action.

The object of his discussion was floating above the Westminster Bridge admiring its surroundings. He had finally honed down the number of bridges he had initially thought to use down to two: Tower bridge and Westminster Bridge but he just couldn't decide between the two, both were important and both were iconic. Time was running short and he needed to make a decision. What on earth was the matter with him, he thought, *I am turning into an indecisive human*. This thought made him laugh.

He looked again at the route the refugee march would be taking and finally made a decision.

The soup kitchen was really busy and Bear had his work cut out keeping up with demand. There was an air of expectancy as small groups of people huddled together on the green. Bear wondered if all the unusual activity had anything to do with the march for the homeless that his wife's mother had talked about. He had never expected that he was ever going to agree with her or even be proud of her but he was. He was surprised at his reaction as he had never got on with her before even though he had tried to.

Roy phoned the following evening to inform his parents that he was coming down for the bank holiday and was bringing a friend with him. Maisie put the phone down having agreed that it was all right for him to bring a friend down with him without asking who the friend was then asked Bear if she had done the right thing. When Bear said she had, she immediately disagreed with him saying Roy should be concentrating on his studies not drifting around with girl or boy friends.

"It will be nice for him to have company on the journey," Bear said as he took Shimmer's lead off of the peg to take her for a walk.

A1 examined Westminster Bridge, happy that he had finally made a choice. Everything was perfect, just too perfect for words. The refugee march was going to end at the houses of parliament which suited him perfectly and, in the end, had made the choice of which bridge to choose easy for him. He decided that he was too soft-hearted as he looked over towards the south side of the bridge at St Thomas' Hospital.

He saw the painted hearts on a wall running alongside the river for the people who had died in the pandemic, surprised by the fact that some humans cared very much about humans and some didn't. He imagined thousands more being painted when his plan came into fruition and curled up laughing. It would be a fitting epitaph.

The closeness of the hospital would be very handy for the few humans who might survive the leap into the Thames, although he hoped that there would be no survivors whatsoever.

A1 admonished himself for making things too hard on himself when, if he had just checked the destination the refugee marchers would be taking, he could have saved himself a great deal of stress. His sphere floated just outside the houses of parliament as A1 stared towards the bridge imagining thousands of screaming human beings leaping off of it into the dirty water of the Thames, landing on top of each other in the process and filling the river with bodies. He would have been surprised that at that very moment he was being closely observed, the thought that it could happen simply never occurred to him.

4Z9 and B4U hovered in the undulating circle approximately fifteen feet away from A1 wondering what he was up to. They deliberately chose the circle to monitor A1 because they knew that A1 was one of the few shadows who could see spheres. Circles on the other hand couldn't be detected by anyone or anything. The shadows knew that the green outside the houses of parliament was the destination of the planned refugee march and guessed that A1's shadows would swell the number of marchers to epic proportions. His shadows would, in fact, be the cuckoos in the nest. 4Z9 and B4U were using the refugee march as a cover for their own ends. What they couldn't work out at the moment was the purpose behind it all, it surely had to be bigger than simply blocking the bridge.

"Why is he looking at the bridge?" 4Z9 asked B4U.

"Perhaps he aims to block it with his homeless humans," B4U offered.

"No, I don't think so," mused 4Z9. "He wouldn't march all this way to simply block a bridge. There must be another card up his sleeve."

"There will be hundreds, perhaps thousands of marchers, they won't all fit on the bridge," offered B4U.

"They need to be careful that they don't push each other off of it into the river," said 4Z9 then stopped. "That's it, that's it." He turned around to look at B4U to see if she knew what he was talking about but she just stared back at him with an uncomprehending look.

"Shadows can't drown!" said 4Z9 excitedly. "Don't you see! Shadows can't drown."

B4U stared at him waiting for him to enlarge on his eureka moment. 4Z9 stared back at her without seeing her as the enormity of what he was thinking struck him. He was suddenly galvanised into action and set a course back to S.A.S. headquarters as he brought B4U up to date.

Back at headquarters, 4Z9 consulted the chief and outlined what he thought A1 was planning. After a lot of discussion as what action to take they prepared for the worst-case scenario as they simply could not stand by and watch thousands of humans perish. The humans in the march had no idea that they were being manipulated and were destined for a watery grave just as they would have no idea when their demise was prevented. Much better to be safe than sorry!

Daisy came out of the soundproofed room and glanced into the garden as she went passed the French doors and saw Mosaic and Shimmer playing in the garden. She stopped and watched her sister for a while wishing that Mosaic was older so that she could have someone of her age to confide in. She knew that she could confide in her mother but some of her fears seemed silly even to herself and there were somethings that you couldn't tell parents! She carried on into the kitchen to see what her mother was baking just as Roy and a friend let themselves into the house. Maisie was covered in flour but threw her arms around her son and hugged him as if she hadn't seen him for months (which she hadn't).

Roy then pulled away and flicked the flour off of his clothes before he introduced his companion to her. "Mum, Geoff. Geoff, Mum," he said then caught sight of his sister. "Oh, and this pretty little one is my little sister, Daisy."

Geoff gave a lop-sided grin and said, "Hello little Daisy," which caused her to flush up and run from the room.

Maisie watched her daughter flee then rinsed her hands off before settling down to catch up on how her son and his friend were doing.

Bear returned a few moments later having gone out at the insistence of his wife to get a haircut. He had toyed with the idea of letting his hair grow long like that of his favourite rock artist but Maisie had soon put paid to that idea. He was carrying a few pot plants as well as a take-away that he had bought on the spur of the moment. No harm done though as the boys had the take-away whilst Bear had the dinner that he knew his wife was cooking but had forgotten about.

During the meal, Bear suddenly said, "Oh, I forgot, I met your mother in the supermarket. Couldn't miss her as she was wearing a bright pink track suit with the legend 'Over sixty—deal with it' emblazoned across the front. She said she was getting supplies for the march tonight though I don't know how she is going to manage to take everything with her, she'll need to take a shopping trolley."

"What march is that then?" enquired Roy.

"It's a march for the homeless and needy though the television said it was a march for refugees," offered Maisie. "Anyway she's got it into her head that she's going and so she's going!"

Roy laughed. "Never thought she would do something like that." Then turned to Geoff and asked, "Shall we go?"

"Don't you dare. I haven' seen you for months and now you are planning to leave when you have only just got here," Maisie said with a catch in her voice then turned to Bear. "Tell them they can't go, tell them."

"I think the lads are big enough to make up their own minds," Bear responded carefully then, seeing her face change he added. "Perhaps they could go just a little way then come back."

Maisie looked from her husband back to her son but pinched her lips together and got up to clear the table. Geoff stood up to help her and Roy and Bear breathed a sigh of relief and managed a tight grin at each other.

That evening, Roy and Geoff accompanied Bear to the soup wagon. When they arrived at the site, they saw that the green in front of the wagon was already crowded with people carrying banners, flags and cardboard slogans, most of which had the legend 'Homes for the homeless' on one side and 'A fair deal for refugees' on the other. The wagon was very busy and the queues of people were unusually chatty. The air was full of expectancy. The boys left Bear and made their way through the crowd after having promised to leave the march if there was any sign of trouble and soon, they were lost in the crowd.

Chapter 23 — 'Homes for the homeless'

A1 floated over the north and south suburbs in the city watching crowds gather. He skimmed over the heads of the gathering marchers reading the banners as he went. The plan was panning out well so far but he knew he shouldn't get complacent. At the signal he had given his shadows had begun to congregate and mix with the 'refugee' marchers whilst displaying the 'A fair deal of refugees' side of their banners.

He had to admit to himself that when the chief had managed to escape from him, he had thought himself incapable of achieving anything again and for a time he became FLR2 again. All that was behind him now, he didn't need the chief or anybody in order to succeed and the proof of that was in what was happening around him at that very moment.

A single voice shouted, "Refugees," and one or two of the crowd responded with, "A fair deal." This was repeated over and over again getting louder and louder as more and more of the crowd joined in until they were letting go and shouting at the top of their voices. Total strangers became friends as they rode the wave of emotion and then, suddenly, without warning, the marchers began to march. Some of the crowd had brought candles with them and others shone torches as they slowly left the green and were swallowed up by the night. Bear looked around himself in amazement, one moment he had been working his socks off and now the field was empty although the sounds of the marchers could still be heard as they slowly made their way through the suburbs towards the heart of the city.

Bear had hoped to see the boys before the marchers left but there had been no sign of them neither had he seen Maisie's mother. From what she had been wearing the other day when he had seen her in the supermarket, he was sure she would be wearing something outlandish. He had a wry smile on his face as he walked back home thinking of her pulling her shopping trolley behind her and shouting slogans at the top of her voice. For a moment he had the urge to join the marchers then the reality of marching through the night hit him and he decided that he was far too old to go gadding about. A warm bed awaited him and he was looking forward to it. The fact that Maisie's mother was years older than him wasn't lost on him but he excused himself, he had a wife and children to consider whereas she lived on her own. He still had an underlying feeling that not joining the march was a cop out though and the feeling stayed with him the rest of the evening.

The headquarters of the S.A.S. was buzzing as ideas were put forward in how to deal with A1. They knew the destination of the refugee march was to the green outside the houses of parliament and took on board 4Z9's idea that the homeless marchers would then continue down the road carrying a lot of the refugee marchers along with them whether they wanted to go or not as they swarmed towards Westminster Bridge. They had to prevent the marchers from reaching the bridge at all costs otherwise all their plans would count for nothing. They also had to take into account that the bridge would be attacked from both sides and not concentrate their forces in one area. They would be foolish to underestimate A1.

One of the S.A.S. members put forward the idea that they should activate the remote device that had been attached to A1's sphere as without him in charge they thought that the march would simply fizzle out. B4U disagreed saying that from the reports coming in from the shadows of birds and trees the march was well under way from both the north and south sides of the city. The march of the refugees was legal, it was only when the march split and tried to invade the bridge that they could intervene. The removal of A1 wouldn't make the slightest difference to the outcome that they perceived.

The opinion B4U put forth swayed a lot of the S.A.S. members and they decided that they would block the attempt by the marchers to get onto the bridge by crowding it with shadows that they had released from the container depot. The shadows would be released on the condition that they could have their freedom if they did as instructed. Some of the members disagreed with this ploy as they said that most of the shadows held in the container depot were criminals and would agree to anything to gain their freedom but in the end, they agreed that even if some of them did their own thing they would still have enough shadows to block the bridge.

4Z9 then took the stage and said that when the human marchers approached the bridge, they would see it was empty and not understand why the march was slowing down and coming to a standstill, whereas their shadows would see that there was no room to move onto it as it was crowded with shadows so they would simply stop their humans from moving forward as they had no place to go. 4Z9 said that A1 was, at the moment, following the marchers from the suburbs in the east side of the city and would be in the location when the marchers arrived at the bridge and would be bound to take some form of action when the marchers failed to storm the bridge. The disruption of his master plans could well cause A1 to react involuntarily so the S.A.S. had to hold their nerve as well as their positions and be prepared for any eventuality. He suggested that S.A.S. members be placed at the north and south sides of the bridge as their reputation would precede them and prevent A1's shadows from attempting to storm the bridge when commanded to do so by A1. An option was put forward that there was no point in crowding the bridge with released shadows as the S.A.S. could prevent the marchers reaching their destination by themselves but 4Z9 squashed the rising sounds of approval of this idea by saying they would be foolish to think that they could prevent the bridge invasion by themselves, they weren't invincible, no organization was. Having the released shadows tightly packed on the bridge was a good back-up plan and that any S.A.S. member who thought that he was a super hero had better leave now as there was no place in the force for that type of thinking!

A1 would have been delighted to be the subject of their conversation. At this moment he was floating along with the marchers as they waved their banners and shouted their slogans. He noticed that there was a police presence along the route and congratulated himself on being the genius he was to have infiltrated the refugee march. He noticed that there were television cameras along the route and amused himself by waving and bowing towards them as he passed although he knew that they couldn't see him.

A1 decided that he was going to make the most of the moment so that he could look back and enact his path to glory. He drove the sphere to the back of the marchers pleasantly surprised at their number. He floated above their heads and shouted out their slogans with them then changed the word 'refugees' to 'A1' and thought himself very clever. He mused over the idea whether he should go and oversee the other marchers coming up from the south of the city or whether he should join those marchers from the north and west but decided he didn't need to, after all, his plan was fool proof and anyway he was enjoying himself too much where he was to bother. There was absolutely no reason for him to go chasing about.

Dawn was chasing the darkness from the sky as the marchers approached their destination hoping to have a chance to rest before the speakers started their discourses. Their chants had almost stopped during the blackest hours of the night but now they were chanting with renewed vigour.

It took A1 a little while to realise that the march had slowed to a snail's pace but he wasn't unduly worried as he travelled towards the front of it singing his praises at the top of his voice. He planned to hover above the Westminster Bridge so that he could have the best view as the foolish humans jumped to their deaths like lemmings from the bridge. He noticed a lot of children in the march as he floated above them and just thought, *the more the merrier*.

B4U had been monitoring A1's position and warned the S.A.S. of his impeding approach. Meanwhile, the marchers who were there to protest on behalf of refugees found themselves swept along as A1's shadows propelled their humans down towards Westminster Bridge. Very few of the refugee marchers managed to extricate themselves as the crowd swamped them like a tidal wave and carried them forwards.

A1 hovered just outside Westminster Station trying to take on board what was happening or rather what was not happening. The march had come to a standstill perhaps twenty feet away from the bridge.

"Come on, come on," he urged them as he floated towards the front of the march. When he saw the cause of the stoppage, he immediately knew he had been foiled. Westminster Bridge was crowded almost to overflowing with hundreds, perhaps thousands, of shadows and as if that wasn't enough S.A.S. troops guarded the entrance in front of him.

A1 screamed, "No, no, no!" He took in the scene before him then, without a rational thought, drove his sphere down onto the bridge cutting a swathe, back and forth, through the shadows on it. He wanted to drive them all away from the bridge but when he rose above the bridge to see what impact he had had he saw that he had had no impact whatsoever. He knew that shadows couldn't be destroyed but his anger was so great that he just had to smash into them time and time again. A1 continued screaming, unable to accept that his plan, his master plan, was failing. He wanted to erase all of the shadows on the bridge but knew that there were just too many of them for him to cope with. He flew to the south entrance of the bridge but saw the same stand-off. He punched the activation button time and time again and a brief hope arose in him as he saw attempts from some of the marchers to move forward in response to his signal.

On the ground, some of the humans towards the front of the marchers saw the empty bridge in front of them and tried to storm it in response to the signal A1 was sending out despite being confronted with the S.A.S. whilst shouting and encouraging the crowd behind them to push forwards with them. The S.A.S. simply erased the shadows of the leading humans who had surged forwards but all that the surrounding crowd saw was a group of perhaps thirty people falling to the floor as if suddenly taken ill.

Somehow the television crews reached the front of the march in order to capture what was happening. Those marchers at the front of the crowd braced themselves against the surge then screamed at the crowd to stop but unfortunately many people were trampled on as the momentum of the crowd carried them forwards. Some people began to help the humans that had fallen in front of them and then there was a brief silence, as if waiting for a sign, before the marchers began to draw away in the opposite direction.

4Z9 watched the marchers turning back and was informed that the same event was happening on the south side of the bridge. B4U told him that A1 had been hovering over the centre of Westminster Bridge but had since moved away. 4Z9 gave the command for the remote-control button that had been placed on the outside of the sphere to be enabled as he didn't want to miss the opportunity of dealing with A1 once and for all. There was no way he was going to underestimate A1 and allow him to escape, for who knows what plan he would come up with next. The erased shadows of the humans who had tried to move against them had been sent back to the holding depot. He watched as their humans were helped to their feet and led away knowing that they would feel strange without their shadows.

A1 had stared down in disbelief at the scene that was unfolding below him, the picture of success in his mind gradually being replaced by the knowledge of failure. Somehow his master plan was flawed, his incredible master plan that had been going to turn him into a legend above legends was incredible no more… The name Charlie came to his mind and he suddenly knew who to blame for his failure. He had known it, he had sensed it, yet he had done nothing about his feelings. Why, oh, why hadn't he got rid of Charlie when he had the chance! Full of unbridled fury and totally unable to think rationally, he set his sphere's co-ordinates to the house of Charlie's human. If he was going to fail, he was going to take Charlie down with him!

It was still early morning and Charlie, R45N, DRT4 and ZUP2 were returning from their classes. Charlie was in the lead looking forward to the day when suddenly everything went black. He felt he was being sucked along a tube at a tremendous speed but could do nothing to stop himself. He was spinning faster and faster as he travelled accompanied by a frightening roaring and hissing sound. As suddenly as it had started the noise and spinning stopped and Charlie found himself in a huge container which held many other shadows. He couldn't move and realised he was being held in a vacuum. It seemed quite a long time before Charlie realised what had happened to him though in reality it was only a few moments, he had been erased he was sure of it. He shouldn't be here surely; everyone knew that once a shadow was erased, they ceased to exist. Charlie didn't know exactly where he was but for the moment didn't care as he slowly recovered from his ordeal.

A1 laughed gleefully, if he was going down, he was glad that he had destroyed the shadow who had caused him to fail.

"Think you can get the best of me do you, huh? Well you had better think again."

A1 didn't know what was happening. He was pinned to the floor of the sphere by the force of the speed it was travelling as it went higher and higher up into the atmosphere. As suddenly as it had started it stopped and A1 found that he could move again. He looked around himself then upwards out of the sphere and saw only darkness. He was confused, still feeling the after effects of travelling at speed. He then looked down and could see the blue and white planet earth turning slowly beneath him and for a while he was mesmerized.

One moment he had been floating above Charlie's house having just erased him and now here he was orbiting the earth. How on earth had it all happened so quickly? A1 examined the thought he had had, orbiting the earth, he was orbiting the earth! He started to scream, and once started couldn't stop himself. In all he screamed for ten human years though as a shadow who lived for ever the amount of time was meaningless.

R45N sent a vibration to 4Z9 to let him know that Charlie had been erased. She had no idea that shadows could never be wiped out, and there was no reason for her to know otherwise. As far as she was concerned Charlie did not exist any more and she was filled with grief. She had no idea as to how the shadows of the household were going to cope as Charlie had always been the linchpin.

It took many hours for the marchers to disperse but the S.A.S. stayed vigilant throughout until it was all right for them to return to headquarters and evaluate what had happened. The shadows that had crowded together on the bridge disappeared as if by magic, many of them feeling a lot wiser than they had been when they were released onto the bridge, and even if some of them didn't want to help the human race they didn't want to hinder it either.

Back at headquarters many of the S.A.S. were shocked that 4Z9 had been proved right but, at the same time, knew that they had achieved a major victory. The humans in general would never know of the catastrophe that had been avoided but that was just how the shadows wanted it. Keeping a low profile and working to promote the well-being of humankind whilst keeping rogue and criminally minded shadows in check was all that mattered to them. No point in thanking them, they were only doing their job after all.

Roy and Geoff were thankful to get back to the green from where their part of the march had started and then walked home to find that Bear was still in bed and sound asleep whilst Maisie was on her mobile to her mother but kept getting no reply. Maisie had spent a long time that morning trying to rouse Bear but when she finally had, he had simply stumbled around in a confused state and in the end, Maisie told him to get back to bed as she thought that he was coming down with something. Bear did not need telling twice and dived thankfully under the duvet and was fast asleep within minutes. Maisie and the girls had all been listening to the news about the march and were relieved when the boys turned up but alarmed when they said that they had no idea where her mother was. In the end Maisie decided to return to the green with Roy and wait until her mother showed up whilst the girls remained with Bear and Geoff. Whilst waiting by the green Maisie received a phone call and found that her mother had fallen ill on the march but had been taken to the nearby St Thomas' Hospital and was doing all right. Whilst listening to the news with the girls she had heard that some of the marchers at the front of the march had suddenly fallen ill but had had no idea that her mother was one of those people.

In the meantime, 4Z9 had left for the container depot and had found Charlie floating in its confines along with hundreds of other shadows. He knew that when shadows first arrived in the container, they were mostly left for a certain amount of time to recover from their ordeal before they were put through the procedures that returned them to serving humans. Although he knew that fact, 4Z9 had to admit to himself that he had been worried that Charlie might have already been processed and assigned to a new human being.

Charlie was relieved to see 4Z9 and told him what it had felt like being erased. 4Z9 asked Charlie if he wanted to go back to his human or if he wanted the chance to serve a different human. Charlie was horrified and said that he wanted to return to his human more than anything as he realised that he totally loved his human and wanted to spend as much time as he could with him. He now understood why 37 had been so upset when his human had died and although his human hadn't died, he was sure that his feelings were similar to what 37's had been.

4Z9 told Charlie that there was a problem with his returning as all the shadows from the household would realise that being erased didn't mean that shadows were wiped out of existence. They would all have to swear an oath to keep the knowledge to themselves and never mention it again, even to each other. 4Z9 then accompanied Charlie back to his human and told him to get attached but encourage his human stay sleeping for a while and Charlie was only too happy to do so.

It was mid-morning when Maisie phoned home to check that everybody was all right. Geoff told her that Bear had just got up and seemed fine and moments later, she was talking to him and explaining that she and Roy were going up to the city to visit her mother who had fallen ill on the march and not to worry. On arrival at the hospital they found that although her mother seemed physically none the worse for wear apart from some bruising she was in a confused state of mind and didn't initially recognise her daughter. The hospital said that they were going to keep her in overnight just to be on the safe side, so Maisie and Roy sat with her until she drifted off to sleep then booked into a nearby b&b.

R45N and RZ2R finally left Maisie and Roy sleeping and went back to the hospital in search of 88T to find out what was happening but her mother's shadow was nowhere to be found. They split up with RZ2R going up to the seminars to ask for help whilst R45N searched for 4Z9.

4Z9 met up with R45N and listened patiently to her story then went with her to the holding depot to see if they could spot 88T and found that the shadow had just been syphoned off from a container in order to be debriefed. The reunion with R45N was joyful but took on a serious edge as 4Z9 explained that neither of them could be allowed to return to their humans unless they swore not to divulge the fact that erasure wasn't a closure. Both the shadows solemnly swore to the fact and 88T swiftly returned to her human.

The following day when Maisie and Roy returned to the hospital, they met a transformed person. Maisie's mum was as right as rain and was allowed home. Maisie phoned home to check the girls were all right then started the journey home with her mother and Roy.

Maisie's mum talked excessively all the way home but Maisie was so pleased that her mother was well that she didn't stop her. Maisie asked her mother what had actually happened to her that she had had to be taken to hospital.

"I had worked my way to the front of the march as I always like to know where I'm going and be in the front if I can. We turned into the road leading to Westminster Bridge and the traffic simply stopped, as if by magic to let us through. Now when do you ever see that?" She paused for breath, and she turned to look at them then continued, "We could see that the road ahead was clear as we waved our banners and shouted, 'Homes for the homeless' at the top of our voices." Maisie's mother suddenly stopped talking as if thinking what to say next, then said, "It was so strange, there we were marching along when we suddenly stopped as if we had hit a brick wall. I kept trying to move forward but my body just wouldn't respond."

"Perhaps you were tired, after all it was rather a long walk," Roy offered.

Maisie's mother had given him a withering look and continued speaking as if she hadn't been interrupted, "The crowd kept pushing us from behind and then suddenly I could move and along with other people, I marched forward then felt nauseous and dizzy. I couldn't see, everything just went black." She stopped speaking and shuddered but said no more. Maisie put an arm around her mother's shoulders and hugged her for all she was worth and the rest of the journey was made in silence.

Chapter 24 — Try, try, and try again!

Just as abruptly as he had started screaming, A1 stopped and started to think about how he had been sent out into orbit. The only solution he could think of was that somehow a remote device had been put in his sphere though he initially found it hard to believe as he never left his sphere. Never ever. No, wait minute, that was not strictly true, he did leave his sphere on occasions when he went inside buildings to glean information but only once had he left it with the hatch open. That was the time that that stupid dog had stopped him from returning to it and he had to go underground for a while.

A1 began to blame himself for being so stupid as to leave his sphere at all as there was no need for him to have left it in the first place. He could have just floated past the house and seen inside it as well as hear everything that was being said if anyone was there! Why oh, why had he left his sphere.

He knew why. It was his saboteur pushing him to take risks that he didn't need to take. Floating in front of the Prime Minister, members of royalty or the chief of police and mimicking them gave him no end of satisfaction.

A1 was asking himself questions he already knew the answer to and was going round in circles. He had to be honest with himself and admit his weaknesses if he was going to make progress of any sort. He had gone into the house where Charlie lived because he could and that was as near to the truth as he could get. He had wanted to invade Charlie' space and see what emanations he could pick up from the house. The fact that he had wasted his time and hadn't picked up any emanations at all was now painfully obvious to him.

A1 realised that his saboteur was rising within him and quickly searched for something to do to prevent it. Find the remote device, yes, yes, that was it. He should stop blaming himself and find the remote device that must have been planted somewhere inside the sphere. He began a painstaking search.

Bear walked slowly down the aisle holding Daisy's hand and smiling fondly at her. She was wearing a beautifully crafted wedding dress the faintest shade of pink with a headdress made up of pink carnations and frothy white flowers that he didn't know the name of. All too soon the walk was over and Bear handed his daughter's hand to Geoff then stepped backwards.

Daisy turned and looked behind her at her bridesmaids and whispered 'thank you' then looked over to her mother who was busy dabbing at her eyes with a dainty lace handkerchief. Just beyond her mother stood her big brother Roy, who was standing with a protective arm around his wife, Suzanne, who was eight months pregnant. Daisy then returned her gaze to Geoff who was gazing down at her. She closed her eyes and took a deep breath, this was the happiest moment of her life.

Mosaic, one of two bridesmaids smiled back at her sister then looked across at Anne, the other bridesmaid and smiled at her. They had become firm friends at veterinary college and their relationship had blossomed into a partnership although they were putting off getting married until they had both qualified as vets. Both bridesmaids were wearing pale pink trouser suits that had been chosen by Daisy.

The reception was exceptional with choices of food to suit all palates. All too soon the reception was over Bear and Maisie returned to their home and for a moment felt lost without Daisy being there, the house, their home, suddenly felt huge. They hugged just inside the front door then Maisie went to put the kettle on whilst Bear let Sparkle, a beautiful black and white Staffordshire bull terrier, out into the garden. Shimmer had passed away peacefully a few years before and they had found that the house was empty without her exuberant presence. Sparkle had been rescued from a puppy farm and was full of energy and love and fitted in to the household straight away.

Charlie was talking to R4T+, Sparkle's shadow, explaining what had happened at the wedding that day but Sparkle wanted to hear all about A1, so Charlie relayed the story as he knew it before R4T+ went off to classes. Charlie and R45N then left for their classes and chose to attend one called 'Erasure. What is it and why is it necessary'? Charlie already knew what erasure was and what it felt like and didn't really want to attend the class but he allowed R45N to persuade him to attend and in the end he was glad he did as it helped to give him some closure.

A1 imagined the S.A.S, or whoever it was who had caused him to be in orbit around the earth laughing at him and the thought didn't go down too well with him. Here he was, the greatest shadow that had ever been created thrust out of the way like he was a nobody. He reflected briefly on what had happened to try and understand where he had gone wrong and yes, he had to admit it, he had gone wrong somewhere, but where! His wonderful plan had been fool proof and he definitely hadn't told anyone anything (not that he had anyone to tell)! He didn't like where his thoughts were going and decided that he should concentrate instead on the positive things that he had achieved.

A1 laughed as he pictured Charlie's face just before he had erased him. He had thought Charlie was the brains behind trying to trap him though he had since been proved wrong as his sphere was thrust skywards after he had erased Charlie.

He still had no idea as to the identity of his enemy or enemies though he had spent many hours trying to work out just who they were. Who was the spy in the camp? He had needed something to concentrate on when his situation had threatened to overwhelm him but still could not come up with an answer other than the chief, the shadow he had absorbed. He reasoned that the chief was the only shadow who was anywhere near him in expertise.

He had wanted to become a legend and now he would be but for the wrong reasons, shadows everywhere would hear his story, hear how close he had come to causing the greatest catastrophe the country had ever experienced. A1 didn't mind them hearing that part of his story for it gave him a mastermind status, it was the next part of the story where he had been sent off to cavort about space as if he was of no consequence that upset him.

Chapter 25 — How time flies!

Bear and Maisie renewed their wedding vows then decided it was time for them to move to a smaller property. Bear had lived in the house all of his life and was both sad and glad to be thinking about moving on. Sad because he had seen some wonderful times in the house but glad because they were both getting on and the house was now far too big for their needs and abilities. Maisie's mother had died a few months previously and it was her passing that had caused the couple to feel unsettled. Maisie wanted to move to Wales as the father she had never seen had been Welsh but in the end, they moved to a place called Mousehole down on the South Coast. Sparkle loved it down there, especially the eye-catching countryside and the long walks on the beach.

A1 was confused. He had gone over every inch of the inside of the sphere twice and he had found nothing at all. He had expected to find something very easily and now that he had nothing to show for his efforts he didn't know where to go next, not that he could choose to go anywhere else. Here he was stuck in a sphere orbiting the earth. He wondered if what he was looking for was camouflaged as something else, for he had decided that that was what he would have done if he had done it to someone else. He went over everything again with this in mind but still came up empty-handed.

"You stupid, stupid idiot. You're a mastermind! You are no more than a master fool." A1 suddenly stopped berating himself when a new thought slid into his mind. If he couldn't find the remote device inside the sphere, then it must be on the outside. Some crafty shadow must have placed it on the outside of the sphere. Here he was thinking his sphere had been entered when he had left it but the crafty sods had placed a device on the outside of it. Clever, very, very, clever, in fact genius. Even he had been misled for a time.

Thinking he had solved part of his problem at least A1 reached for the lever to open the sphere door. Just as he was about to use it, he stopped, wait a minute, wait a minute. If he was in space, and he was, then there would be no air outside of his sphere, it would be like he was inside a vacuum, unable to move! He hurriedly moved away from the lever realising that he had come very close to ending all hopes of escaping. He would have spent eternity floating about in space, able to see what was happening to him but unable to move and worst of all he would have been a victim of his own accusations against himself. Nobody could berate him worse than he could.

For a long time A1 did nothing, it was as if he was enacting what would have happened to him if he had opened the sphere door. Thoughts of events that had happened to him during his existence gradually filtered into his mind and he began to remember the skills he had gained when he had been assigned to a telegraph pole in the middle of nowhere. He was a shapeshifter, now, how could that ability help him to escape from the predicament he was in?

If he made himself into a cannon ball and travelled back and forth horizontally across the sphere, perhaps he could jolt the sphere out of orbit. He decided that the idea wouldn't work, after all he wasn't sure how robust the sphere was, supposing it cracked!

Supposing, he thought, that he made the sphere a giant cannonball, surely the weight of it would pull him back down to the earth! Before he could transform a new idea came into his mind, what if he transformed himself into a gigantic magnet, now surely that was plausible!

Years passed as A1 tried one thing after another. He wouldn't give up although he did stop every now and then to give vent to bouts of screaming whilst in the midst of total despair. In order not to focus on his predicament he spent a very long time going through his master plan trying to be brutally honest with himself and admit where he had made mistakes so that he wouldn't make them the next time around.

The next time, oh yes. He knew that he had to think positively, he would succeed in getting back to earth, and when he had discovered about the mistakes he had made, he would unleash a master plan that made his failed plan look feeble.

He wondered if he turned himself into a satellite dish if he could beam himself down to earth or at least set up a vibration which he could return to earth on. He was sure that he was on the right track and was very hopeful about this thought.

Charlie still attended classes continuing to look for ways to help his human become enlightened. He was at that very moment talking to 4Z9 who had asked him to think about becoming a full-time S.A.S. member when his human passed on. Charlie said thank you but no thank you as if his human hadn't fulfilled what he was meant to fulfil in this lifetime, he wanted to see if he could be his shadow in his next life and help him get enlightened in that one.

"Supposing your human does go on up to heaven and doesn't return, what then?"

"Then I want to become a shadow to a wolf."

"Still want to shadow a wolf?"

"Yes, I do. I feel a strong affinity with them."

"Really!"

"Yes, really. They are endangered because some of humanity sees them as a threat and persecute them. Wolves have as much right as any life force on earth to live their lives free from persecution."

"You know that wolves have a high-risk of being killed and yet you still want to become a shadow to one?"

"More than anything," responded Charlie.

"Well the offer still stands," said 4Z9. "After all, we have all the time in the world. The chief has come up with the idea of some shadows working full-time with the human police helping them to solve their crimes. He is still working on the finer details but perhaps in time we may find ourselves working side by side."

There was silence between the shadows for a little time then Charlie said, "What of A1?"

"He's orbiting the earth."

"I almost feel sorry for him."

"Don't. I dread to think what would have happened if his plan had succeeded."

"What of the homeless people and the refugees. Now that my human has moved out of the area, I don't get to see the homeless people so much. I do see a lot of refugees though."

"I don't know so much about refugees I must admit but I am sorry to say that I believe that there always will be homeless people."

"Why do you say that! That's awful."

"Many people get into the mindset that because there have always been homeless people there always will be homeless people, and don't forget that some people actually prefer to be homeless, they don't want to conform or to be shaped by the society they live in. Some prefer to live in the shadows of society!"

"No. I don't believe that for a minute."

"Well, that's as maybe. We can only do our best for them."

"How can we help them?"

"By doing what you are doing now, looking after your human the best way you can and reporting to us any shadows who don't have humans and any humans who don't have shadows."

"You don't have a human."

"Members of the P.A.T.H. and S.A.S. squads don't need to have humans," 4Z9 responded then added, "they can't be erased either."

"Really!"

"Yes, really."

"Will A1 ever be able to get back down to earth, I mean is it possible that he could?"

4Z9 looked at Charlie then said, "It is possible. Anything is possible if you try hard enough. We can never underestimate what he is capable of."

Charlie was incredulous. "It is possible! You mean he could be down here even now plotting his comeback."

4Z9 responded, "Even if A1 doesn't 'make a comeback there will always be a shadow out there looking to fill his boots so to speak."

Charlie changed the subject. "How is ZUP2 getting on?"

"He's doing really well, one to look out for. How is the shadow that replaced him doing?"

"You mean X81?"

"Yes. X81."

"Doing really well although the human Daisy went through a bit of a rough patch soon after the time he transferred to her."

"No, really!"

"Yes, she had a miscarriage a few months after X81 took over from ZUP2."

"How awful."

"Well nobody said that looking after a human was easy. They are a very complicated species. There are billions of them and they are all different!"

"What would they do without us."

"Yes, what indeed."

The End